RESISTING DYLAN

COWBOY INSPIRED ROMANCE

SOPHIA SUMMERS

ACKNOWLEDGMENTS

Thank you Emily Flynn for your helpful insight into this book. Your instincts are right on. Much gratitude to all my readers. I hope this books inspires as much as it entertains.

READ ALL BOOKS BY SOPHIA SUMMERS

JOIN HERE for all new release announcements, giveaways and the insider scoop of books on sale.

Cowboy Inspired Series
Coming Home to Maverick
Resisting Dylan
Loving Decker

Her Billionaire Royals Series:
The Heir
The Crown
The Duke
The Duke's Brother
The Prince
The American
The Spy
The Princess

Read all the books in The Swoony Sports Romances
Hitching the Pitcher

CHAPTER 1

*D*ylan's horse, Pepper, quivered beneath him. They waited for the buzzer. Dylan crouched forward. Pepper's weight shifted. The buzzer sounded, and they raced out into the arena after the calf. He lifted his rope into the air. It circled once, twice, then soared out after the calf. It met its intended mark, circling the horns. He leapt from his horse, used the tie rope to wrap the hooves, and stood while Pepper dragged the calf away. His gaze centered on the time board while the extras untied the calf and let it go. Low scores. High time. He walked back across the arena after Pepper, trying not to kick at the dirt in frustration.

His boss, Trev, waited.

"I know."

"Those are still national scores, but not winning. Not Olympic."

"I know."

Dylan kept walking. The man followed.

"I'll work on drills." Dylan's mind was spinning in a painful repetition about all the things he could do to try and bring down his time.

"That's not gonna do a dang thing."

He turned to face his coach. "Then what do you want from me? I got nothing else, Trev."

"Figure out your head."

"My head?" He turned, disbelieving. Was this some kind of shrink chat?

"Something's off in here, Dylan." The old guy, famous for his own rodeo wins, tapped his temple. "Until you fix it, nothing else is gonna go right."

He nodded, and the man let him be. Dylan worked on Pepper for an hour, brushing down his coat, checking his hooves, and life started to fall back into focus. So Trev wanted him to work on what was messing with him on the inside? He tossed the brush back into the bin. There wasn't a dang thing he could do about that mess. Unless of course his boss knew of a way to get his girlfriend to fall back in love with him.

Trev had been single for years. Dylan guessed he was not the one to ask.

After showering off, Dylan had nowhere to go, nothing to do, and no one to do it with. He sat back on his couch in the tiny trailer and put his stockinged feet up on the table, hearing his mama's disapproval in his head as he did so. He reached for the remote to turn on his television but then stopped. On the shelf above the remote, under a T-shirt he'd thrown up there and on top of a pile of magazines, sat his Bible. He could see the dust that had collected on its surface. The worn edges, the smudged coloring on the gilded pages, and the soft leather were also visible. And a part of him wanted to sink deep into those words like he wanted nothing else. A sharp hunger filled him, and he reached for the word of God.

The book fell open for him, on a chapter he'd read a hundred times. He skipped ahead, not wanting the comfort of Psalms praises. He needed some butt-kicking, and the Bible could do that like nobody's business. Perhaps God could help him know how to get out of his rut.

He tried thinking about Shelby. "How can I win that girl back?" But that felt all kinds of wrong. Yes, he wanted her back in his life. But for some reason that question just wasn't a God thing right now. "How can I fix my messed-up head?" He laughed at himself. This wasn't a game. But he really did need some help. Maybe he'd just read. Read and read and read until he felt better. He nodded, lifting the book closer to his face, and began in John.

"In the beginning was the Word, and the Word was with God, and the Word was God." As the words settled around him and through him, the beginnings of peace joined him. "In him was life; and the life was the light of men. And the light shineth in darkness; and the darkness comprehended it not." Truth. His breath slowed and tension left.

Perhaps there was some of this that really didn't matter at all? Maybe he could just let it go for now—all the irritation, the loneliness. Maybe God hadn't left him.

He kept reading. He would just look for that light. He'd see it around him. Maybe a path would open. "He came unto his own, and his own received him not." Not very comforting for Dylan, but something very clear reached him and touched him at his center. God had not been given a free ride. He'd had it tougher than any of them, tougher certainly than Dylan. And He'd continued to do what was required. He did His job, loved every one of them, and stayed the course until he was finished.

Dylan closed the Bible. He was not altogether hopeful but… challenged, humbled. Perhaps he didn't have much to be moping over after all.

He wanted to pray. But he hadn't done that in so long, and he had been so upset by all the prayers left unanswered that he'd sort of given up praying. He wasn't sure now was the time to start. So he left it at a wanting. God would hear. He would know. He wiped the dust from his Bible and placed it on his bed. Then he picked up the phone. He was gonna give his mama a call. They'd be gathering for Sunday dinner, and if he skipped out, he'd hear about it. Besides, there was nothing like reading the Bible to get him thinking about home.

Mama answered and immediately started talking to what he assumed was a room full of his family. He imagined Mama waving her hands around for everyone to hush. Almost everybody he loved most would be in that room. Gracie, his brother's daughter, was playing tug the rope with two overly large rescue dogs that she had convinced the entire Dawson family were necessary. That girl had a smile that could win over any resistant soul.

The sounds of home filled his ear through the phone. Plates were landing on the large wood table. He closed his eyes to see the picture of his father, arm around his mother, up on the wall. His chest tightened. He still missed him. How many rodeos had Dylan won, standing with a medal, wishing his dad could have seen him?

Mom was in full meal mode. Did she even have the phone by her ear anymore? "Mama?" He had lost his mother. She was now directing placement of the roast. "Mama?"

When she didn't answer, he knew he'd lost her to all the distractions in their full farm house on a Sunday night. A familiar ache spread. "Tell everyone I love them."

"Oh, don't you be hanging up yet. We got a surprise for you."

He waited while his mama muffled the phone, her voice still clear to his ears. "Move the chairs so people can get by. I've got Dylan. We're just waiting for Maverick." She tsked. "Where is that boy?"

"Boy, she calls him. I'm pretty sure he's as man as anyone." Nash's slow drawl made Dylan smile. Nash was the youngest, and he got away with the most. But Gracie loved her uncle, and so did the rest of them.

"Dylan, honey, you still there?"

"Yes, I'm here—"

"Get those dogs out of here. Gracie, I'm sorry, but they're just gonna have to play outside."

Then everything quieted. "Okay, we're ready. Dylan, you're on speaker now."

"Hi, everyone."

Various greetings made him smile. He really had no idea what the big announcement might be. He was just calling home to check in during family dinner as expected every week. If any Dawson couldn't be there, they touched base. It was the Dawson way. And he had a bit of news himself.

"Bailey, I'll let you take it from here."

Bailey and Maverick had been married a couple years now, dated for lots before that with a glitch in the middle. Maybe he and Shelby's relationship was just in a glitch.

Bailey tapped a spoon on a cup. When people quieted again she laughed. "You all know that we've been trying to bring Grace some siblings."

Dylan's throat tightened. He had a lot, and he would be considered blessed by most, but what he wanted most was right there in Bailey and Maverick's life. A family of his own, children.

"We found out we're not going to have a baby."

The room was silent, and Dylan's stomach dropped. *Oh no.*

"We're going to be having two!"

He laughed out loud. "What!" Two! Twins?" He wished for his twin in that moment like he'd lost an arm. "Decker, you hear that?"

No one could hear him. He was a phone on the table while everyone hugged and laughed and cheered. He could hear them all fussing over Bailey and teasing Maverick. Then his phone dinged with an incoming text.

His throat tightened. It was Decker. *"Dude, can you believe it!"*

"Hey D. Awesome. Some more Dawson twins."

"Does that mean we're not original?"

"Oh, we're original. THE Dawson twins. They're ANOTHER set of Dawson twins."

"Right. Cool. Miss you bro."

"Yeah. You too. Maybe I'll try to fly home in between the next two." He suddenly wanted that more than anything.

"Do it. Let's go fishing."

"Still trying to catch one bigger?" He snorted. It was their tired comfortable conversation. It felt like home more than anything.

"Not trying. My last one beat your record."

"No picture. No fish."

"Duude."

His mom got back on. "Dylan? Are you there?"

"Yes, I'm here."

"Did you hear that?"

"Yes! Another Dawson set of twins!"

"When you put it like that, maybe we should leave town until they're all grown." Maverick's overly happy voice made Dylan smile.

"You afraid I'm going to corrupt your kids?" Dylan laughed.

Mama's voice came back close to his ear. "Of course he's not thinking that. His kids will be blessed with all of you in their lives. Your father would be so pleased."

There was a respectful pause, as always, after any mention of their father. They missed him every day. The sharpness of the pain was gone, but again, the ache in his chest grew.

"When are they due?" It was killing Dylan not to be there to get all the news.

"Oh! I don't even know." His mama muffled the phone again. "Bailey, when are they coming?"

Her voice returned, louder this time. She forgot she wasn't speaking to the room. "May! They'll be here in May. Oh, what a Christmas you'll have, darlin'. All growing with child, like

Mary herself." Mama sighed. "I carried Nash at Christmas time."

"Yep. That's why she loves me best."

"Oh hush. I don't love anyone best."

"Don't listen to her. She loves Nash best." Maverick's deep voice carried across the room.

"Oh, you. Stop." Dylan imagined his mother trying to swat Maverick with a kitchen towel.

"We all know she loves Gracie best." Nash made Dylan laugh. He was not lying. Gracie had stolen his mom's heart before she was even theirs.

They continued with their fun back-and-forth, and Dylan just listened.

Mama got back on. "Dylan, did you say you have news?"

He rotated his neck. "Nah. My news is nothing compared to that. I'll call you back tomorrow." Winning a place on a national rodeo tour had seemed great at the time, but not compared to the announcement of twins.

"Well now, I'd like to hear it. We all would."

After a second's delay, the room erupted in cheers, and he shook his head at his mom's obvious drumming up of support.

He cleared his throat. "Well, like I just told Mama, we've already heard the best news of today, but yesterday I got the news that I've got a spot on the national tour."

"That's awesome!" Nash was probably standing. He'd be the one most excited about the news anyway, him and Deck.

Nash's voice was in his ear. "Dude, that's so deserved. They finally got smart."

"I'll be doing ropes."

"Perfect. When do they need you?"

"I've got a couple more rodeos, and then I'll go start training again. Probably September."

Mama's voice moved closer. "Then I can expect you at Thanksgiving."

"Absolutely."

"And Christmas. It's gonna be real special this year."

"You can count on it."

"I know. We can always count on you. I'm happy for you, son."

They said their goodbyes. He could tell the group wanted to get on with dinner. He hung up even before they said the prayer. Oh well. It was fine.

Her voice and their love lingered for a moment as he stared at the now dark screen on his phone.

When he hung up from these weekly calls, he usually felt better, filled with a dose of home big enough that he carried it with him for the next few weeks of rodeo competition. But this time when his thumb ended the call, he was left with an ache. What was with this ache? It felt like a hole. It reminded him of all that was missing in his life.

He pulled out his wallet and the old, wrinkled photo of Shelby. He loved her smile. She had been looking at him when the picture was taken. Those were the days they had made promises. When he'd thought that, no matter what happened, they'd be together.

But suddenly she'd gotten this itch. That was the only way he could think to describe it. She was uncomfortable in her own skin. Or uncomfortable in Willow Creek. Uncomfortable with him? He couldn't stand to ask himself that question. But whatever the reason, she'd left. And she hardly talked to him anymore. At least she hadn't run. At least he could still call. At least she hadn't done what Bailey had done to Mav.

And now she lived in New York City. Manhattan. What Willow Creek citizen could be comfortable in New York? Apparently Shelby could, because all he ever heard from her was how awesome it was, and how fun, and how much energy, and did anyone ever sleep? The whole thing exhausted him just thinking about it.

But maybe it was time to pay her a visit. She hadn't asked him to come, not once. She never talked about missing him. They were broken up officially. Maybe she was dating other people. The thought sunk like lead in his gut. But listening to Gracie on the phone, hearing the news of the twins, made him want to take action. Do something. Maybe if she saw him in New York, it would remind her of what they had. Could he stand living there too? Maybe. If that's what it took. He could get an apartment there, travel for rodeo, but see her in between. His mind started working through scenarios of how to make a city life work so they could be together.

He sent her a text. "Hey, babe." He stopped. She didn't like to be called *babe* anymore. He deleted that. "Hey, Bee. I've got a show nearby. Can I come see you this weekend?"

Three dots showed up, but after ten minutes, she still didn't answer. That couldn't be a good sign.

He put his phone in the top of his three drawers of belongings in the trailer he used as a home on the road. Time to go for a ride.

He frowned. At some point he really wanted his companionship to grow beyond his dog Sam and his horse Pepper.

The guys on the team were fine. They were professionals. But he didn't really feel close to any of them.

Time to see if the city life was for him. Maybe that's all she needed...some kind of demonstration from him that he really cared. Maybe this was like one of those romance movies she made him watch. Time for his big gesture, his proof that he really loved her. He'd book a flight for this weekend, and then she'd come running across the airport and fall into his arms, crying in gratitude...yeah right. More like run and hide. Or maybe she'd appreciate him at least. Either way, he had to know.

He purchased plane tickets from his phone while making his way to the stables. Just as he pushed the purchase button, he bumped into someone soft. Her hair tickled his nose.

She giggled.

"Tania." He stepped back, steadying her shoulders with his hands.

"Whatcha doing? You walked right into me." Her smile was large and welcoming.

He dropped his hands, though the skin on her shoulders was soft.

She leaned closer. "Not that I mind."

He tipped his hat. "Sorry about that. Just making a quick purchase." He held up his phone and waited, but she stayed put, right in front of him, looking up into his face.

She was pretty. Her eyes were wide. She'd made it plain as day that she was interested in something. He'd just never explored what that something could be. He couldn't seem to want anyone but Shelby. Even this woman, pretty as anyone, just wasn't the same.

He stepped aside, "Well, you have a good night now."

She put her hand on his arm. "You want some company?"

His eyes widened as he searched her face, lingering a moment until her cheeks colored. "Just what kind of company are you offering? I remember eating apple pie with your mama on nights just like this one."

She looked away. "Oh, just a walk, I guess."

He chuckled, and she looked back up into his face. Then he shook his head. "I've got to get out of my head for a bit. I think all I need is Pepper and a large stretch of land."

"You can't be alone forever, you know. Maybe you just need a quick rebound girl." She swayed her hips, blinking up into his face.

He shook his head and stepped closer.

Her eyes lit with hope.

"You're better than that. You deserve to be much more than anyone's rebound girl."

She looked away again, her lower lip jutting out. Her shoulders drooped. "You're right." She stepped away.

"Tania."

Her half glance was half embarrassed, half hopeful.

"You're a real pretty girl. I know Tommy has been hoping for some attention for months, and he's a real good guy."

She nodded and turned.

Dylan kept walking. Maybe they'd make something special of things. He snorted. Was he a matchmaker now?

There was nothing wrong with dating a girl, taking her out, walking around after hours; but he just couldn't feel anything more for her, and that wasn't fair to anyone. Not now.

Maybe a quick trip to New York would help set his mind straight. Or even better, help set Shelby's heart looking in his direction.

CHAPTER 2

$\mathscr{K}$ate watched her roommate, Shelby, try on a fifth outfit. She would be on call as outfit judge until Shelby walked out the door. They'd already talked about her lipstick color, hair, and shoes. Kate didn't mind. But sometimes she wondered if Shelby would do the same for her, were Kate to ever actually go on a date.

She was too busy for dating, she told herself. Tonight, as soon as Shelby left, she had to start sifting through the slush pile for her agency. As the newest agent, they wanted her to make a real effort to find new authors.

Shelby twirled, her short skirt billowing out around her. "I think this is the winner."

"You look stunning." Kate thought her roommate had looked great in all the previous outfits, too. Shelby was the kind of woman that made everything in the store look like it was fitted just for her. Perfect body type, perfect skin color. And she was super polite and pleasant, so a person couldn't hate her for it. Perhaps self-obsessed might be the best word to describe Shelby. But wasn't everyone, in one way or another?

Shelby studied herself in the mirror. "Yep, I think this is it. And good thing. Ramon is coming in ten minutes." She air-kissed Kate. "I'll see if he has a friend for you. Wouldn't it be great to double?"

"Totally. But not tonight."

"Yes, I know. You have work. Kate, you need to get out more."

She nodded and waved Shelby away, her fingers already itching to tap away on her keyboard.

But then Shelby's phone dinged. "Oh no."

"What is it?" Kate asked.

"Dylan texted."

Kate squinted in concentration.

"The guy from home."

She nodded slowly. Shelby never talked about him. "I didn't think you guys still talked."

"We don't. I mean, we broke up, but he's sort of waiting."

Kate stared at her. "Does he know you're dating? Does he know about Ramon?"

"No, we don't talk. I didn't think I needed to tell him every relationship update." Her thumbs hovered over her phone. "If I told him, maybe he'd move on too."

"Wouldn't that be a good thing?"

Shelby's normally placid face frowned. "I don't know. No." She shook her head. "No. if he moves on…" She shook her head, starting to type a reply. "He would be married tomorrow if he wanted. He's the biggest catch ever. He'll get snatched up immediately."

Kate stared at her roommate. "But again, wouldn't that be a good thing?"

"Not if things don't work out with Ramon." Shelby rolled her eyes and typed faster. "There."

"What?"

"He's coming."

"Wait, here?"

"Yeah, he has this weekend free, so he's coming."

"And Ramon?"

"He'll be fine. Me and Dylan are old friends." She winked. "At least that's all Ramon needs to know."

Kate turned back to her monitor, her foot tapping underneath the kitchen table. The sooner Shelby left for the evening, the better.

"I might need to beg favors while he's here."

Kate lifted her eyes again.

"You know, if I have something going on, you could, like, entertain Dylan for me."

Kate sighed. "Sure. Just let me know what you need."

"Oh, thank you. You're gonna love him. Like I said, he's every woman's dream. Tall, beautiful. Cowboy." She shrugged like he obviously wasn't her dream. "So he won't be any trouble, I'm sure. It would be good for you to get out."

And Kate watched Shelby step out of their tiny apartment. Once the door shut and the apartment was quiet again, she tried to return to the latest book submission in her inbox, but one word bounced around her mind. Cowboy?

Her gaze flicked to the one book she'd brought from home. She wasn't certain why it sat on her shelf, except she couldn't leave it at home. When packing up her room, it came with her. Old slips of paper poked out the top. Page fifty-seven had a soft palomino. Page eighty-two had a black, glistening Arabian with a white diamond on his forehead. Kate knew every page of every one of her favorite horses. Every horse. The book of horse breeds had been her most read, most cherished possession all through high school. It had come with her to college, mostly just as an ornament, but here it sat, one of her very few possessions in New York City.

She pulled it out for the first time in several years and

flipped through the pages. *Cowboy*. What kind of men worked with these magnificent animals? After going through each and every breed she'd marked as a younger girl, she left the book open on the table and reached for her other book she hadn't left at home, her most read, most worn out and loved book.

It landed with a comfortable heaviness in her lap, and she let the pages open where they would. The sound of the thin sheaves falling open, the smell of years of reading, filled her with comfort. This Bible had been a gift to her as a young child and had come right when she was looking for it. She'd always assumed there was a god. But where was he in Kate's life at that time? She wasn't certain. And then her Sunday school teacher gifted her a Bible. Her own one.

She still asked that question sometimes. Where was God in her life? Life didn't always fall into place in the ways she had hoped. All those dreams she had as a child—what purpose had they now? She shook her head and glanced down at the words on the well-worn, well-loved pages. What did God want her to know today?

The book had opened to an odd place in the Old Testament, but she scanned the page anyway. From her experience, there were hidden gems within the Old Testament stories that were incredibly profound. Job 23:12. *Oh Job*. Why did she open up to Job? That man suffered more than any other person in the Bible, save Jesus only. And that was important, for no one shall descend below our Savior. She sighed and winced but read the verses that stood out on the page. "I have not departed from the command of His lips; I have treasured the words of His mouth more than my necessary food."

Kate nodded. That wasn't so bad, And Kate herself thought she'd done just that. Did she not treasure God's word above all else? She thought about it. Is that what it was saying, though? That she preferred reading the Bible to eating? Perhaps. And she certainly enjoyed a good pizza. A hot chocolate with salted caramel or mint at Christmastime. Would she trade it all for the Bible in her life? She shook her head. She didn't need to know such things, for she had both. She was blessed with God's word anytime. And perhaps she would. She could go many days without her favorite hot chocolate, but to go without God's word? Maybe it was just a reminder to put God first. Better keep that in mind.

She sighed and set the Bible back on the shelf, uncertain what she'd learned from the exercise.

Her mind wandered. So, Shelby's hot ex-boyfriend cowboy was coming into town, was he? She pulled up Instagram, scrolling through Shelby's account until it was nothing but a stream of images of her and a dark-haired, tall, tan, good-looking cowboy.

Kate stared and stared. She didn't think they made men like him anymore. At last she turned off her phone and placed it facedown on the table. They *didn't* make men like that anymore. He was not as good as he looked. He couldn't be. And, honestly, a man like that would get eaten alive in New York. And even though she'd carried around this horse book for years on end, New York was her dream. She was finally living her dream, and looking at a boots-wearing, broad-chested cowboy wasn't going to change a single thing.

She forced her attention back to her work, and before she finally turned out the lights, she had gone through and rejected twenty submissions in the slush pile.

Sleep was far from her mind as she let out a long breath and hugged a pillow to her chest, with one thought crowding out all others.

It really would be nice to have someone tall and strong in her life, with a bit of stubble on his chin. Boots would be fine, she decided. As long as he liked New York. Not Shelby's ex-boyfriend obviously, but someone. Maybe Shelby was right, maybe she did need to get out more.

She groaned. "I am never going to get any sleep." After three more restless breaths, she threw on a shirt and her flip-flops, grabbed her purse, and stepped out the door. A walk would do the trick. She'd get rid of every restless thought and then return, craving her pillow.

CHAPTER 3

*D*ylan walked through the crowded Kennedy airport. "Everyone is short."

"What!" Decker was in his ear, and the earbuds made him feel like they were sitting in the room they'd shared as kids.

"They're all short." Dylan felt like he stood at least a foot taller than most people. "And they're in a real hurry."

"Hmm. You know what they say about New Yorkers."

"What?"

"You know. They're in a hurry. They're grumpy. Don't hold them up in traffic or you might get run over."

He laughed. "Do they say that?" He thought about his Shelby. "I can't imagine Shelby even fitting in here." Her white blond hair would stand out like a beacon.

"I don't know. Get her started about something and she might sound like a New Yorker…"

If his brother had been next to him, he would have received a pillow to the face. "Dude. She's not like that."

"Well, in defense of New Yorkers, they're some of the best people around. They're loyal. They work hard. They have a set of rules—if you follow them, you're in. And they're decent people."

Dylan debated the truth of that as a man ran into him and then hurried off without a backward glance. "I hope you're right." That guy had tourist written all over him.

"Well, you're not moving in, are you? You can do anything for a weekend."

Dylan hadn't told anyone that he was considering moving his home base up here to Manhattan. He hadn't told them because he knew what they would say. He'd been shocked at how relieved his family had seemed when Shelby left. "There are a lot of women in the world just like Shelby," his mama had said. "You need to find someone just a bit more." Her loving eyes and tight squeeze had meant to comfort him, but instead he'd felt betrayed. His mama had had opinions about Shelby all this time and not told him? He shook his head. He tried to think back if there were any clues about his mama's dislike. Perhaps.

He exited the airport and approached a line of yellow cabs. He didn't imagine a single Dawson would be pleased about this trip or the thought of him attempting to move to Manhattan.

"Does she know you're coming?"

"Yep." He approached the first cab and got inside. That was easy enough. "Dude, these buildings are so tall you can't see the top from inside your cab."

"You've really never been to New York?" Decker's voice was amazed and just condescending enough that Dylan would have ended the call if he didn't need his brother's help.

"Remember, just use the machine to pay. It's right there in front of you."

"Gotcha." He swiped his card and then leaned back in his seat, trying to take in as much of New York as he could. "How come you didn't stay here if you like it so much?"

"That was just a quick summer internship." Something about

his voice made Dylan wonder if he secretly would have liked to stay.

"You came back so Maverick could do the rodeo."

A puff of breath in Dylan's ear admitted more than his words. "Yeah, sort of. I stayed home 'cause I thought it best. The Dawson Ranch is a business just like all the others in New York. I'm learning and putting to use all that stuff from my business classes to help at home."

"Well, now we're doing great. There's no need for those kinds of sacrifices." Dylan hoped his brother would do whatever it was he wanted.

"Can we talk about you for a second?"

"What?"

"What are you gonna do if she's not really ready for you to be there?"

"What do you mean?"

"Well, what if she's dating someone? What if when she broke up with you, she meant it?"

The pause after he finished that sentence was long and full, but Dylan didn't really know how to answer it. "I don't know. But what if she's hoping for this very thing? What if me coming makes all the difference?"

Decker's sigh lingered. "I guess you won't know until you do it."

"Brother, there's a reason you're my twin."

"Yeah, I know. I get you."

"Try to help the others when they find out."

"Maybe they won't ever know."

"There's a chance." His cab slowed. He thanked the driver and stepped out onto the street, his duffel slung up over his shoulder. People crowded past. "Wow, D, there's a lot of people here."

His twin laughed in response. "Not quite like Willow Creek, is it?"

"Not one bit." He turned, lifting his head up to see the top of his hotel. Shelby's apartment building was next door. That's all that mattered. And she'd said she could get together in the morning. He would just go into the hotel, get his room, get some room service, and plan a breakfast to sweep her off her feet.

But when he was up in his small hotel room, looking out at the alleyway, he couldn't sit, stand, or lie down. A new energy drove him to step back outside and hunt down his dinner.

The crowds were not any less even though it was getting later in the evening. He pulled up his phone and scrolled through all the nearby food options. He wasn't totally paying attention when he walked into someone else.

He glanced up, not really seeing anyone, then stepped into a promising place with a horseshoe on the doorframe.

Inside felt a bit more like home. The walls appeared to be wood, the tables were old, knotty replicas of a typical burger joint in Willow Creek, and the smell... He breathed deeply. Yep. They'd mastered a good healthy mix of barbeque, burgers, fries, and beer. His smile grew.

A soft, short presence at his side bumped against him.

Without looking, he stepped aside to make room.

She sighed. "Sorry."

Something about her voice, the tone, tugged at him.

She was much shorter than he, and as she stared up into his face with her chin lifted, he saw a pair of deep brown eyes. Her nose turned up at the end, and her soft, round face made him smile. She seemed like someone his mama would love to wrap an arm around and show the kitchen. He shook his head. He couldn't be thinking everyone here in Manhattan had all the homegrown manners of Willow Creek. "That's quite all right. I hope I'm not in your way." He stepped further to the side so that she could pass.

But she didn't move. "Go ahead."

So he walked over to the empty hostess stand. She joined him right behind. Then she lifted a menu. "You ever been here before?"

"No, you?"

She shook her head.

"Well, if this is anything like our burger places back home, you want to stick with the original. That burger is bound to be the best."

A hostess arrived. "That's true. We claim to have the best burger in New York." She indicated a wall of signed photographs, presumably all the famous people who had come to stop by.

"Great. I think I'll have one."

Music started from a band in the corner. And they started playing some of Dylan's favorite older country tunes. He wondered if they'd play a Bailey song. Then the whole trip would be meant to be.

When the hostess looked to the woman who stood slightly behind him, her soft voice answered, "Just one."

Dylan turned. "Two. Would you like to join me?"

Her eyes widened, but she seemed pleased. "Yes. I'd like that."

"Great."

The hostess nodded and clicked around on her tabletop monitor before collecting two menus and leading them across a small dance floor into a corner booth. They were in the opposite corner from the band, which made conversation possible, and they had an excellent view of the dance floor.

"This is perfect. Thank you." When they were both settled, he held out his hand to his new dinner partner. "I'm Dylan."

"Kate. Thank you for joining me. I didn't really want to sit alone."

"Turns out I didn't either. So tell me, how long have you been in New York?" He leaned back and rested his arm across the back of the bench. The band started in louder.

Her next words were drowned out.

"Would you mind moving a little closer?" He wiggled his eyebrows, and her eyes widened. Then he laughed. "I'm just kidding. I'm only wanting a friendly chat, but if you don't move closer I won't hear a word you're saying."

Her face turned a fascinating shade of red, and then she moved to sit at his side. His arm was still across the back of the bench. But he left it there to avoid another awkward reshuffling. "So tell me again? How long have you been here?"

"Great. So, I've been here for a couple years. I work for Thompson Literary Agency."

"That's incredible. So do you know any famous authors?"

She laughed. "A few. I'm newer, so I hope that some of the authors I work with will one day be famous." She shrugged and he appreciated her humility.

"And I bet you get to read a lot of amazing books."

"That's true." She sipped her water. "Although today I had to read a lot of really bad ones."

"So people send you bad books?"

"Well, I'm certain they don't think the books are bad, but they just aren't a good fit for our agency."

He nodded. "Interesting. So, tell me the most recent book you read for pleasure."

Her eyes lit, and he knew he'd stumbled onto a subject she would enjoy.

She went on about two of the latest New York Times bestselling books of the week, and her eyes were shining lights. It was amazing how bright two dark-brown eyes could be. When the waiter came back to take their order, Dylan felt like he suddenly knew all about the list and how authors made it and how good those two particular books were.

She shifted in her seat. "I'm sorry I've been going on. Tell me how long you've been visiting."

"Visiting? How did you know I've been visiting?"

She laughed, and he liked the sound. It was real, earthy. Again he thought of their ranch.

"Have you ever been on a ranch?"

She choked. "A what?"

"A working ranch. With cows and horses and hay and land?"

The shake of her head disappointed him. Though that he should care about her ranch experience surprised him.

"Well, that's where I work. Our family owns Dawson Ranch."

"And why aren't you there? Do you have ranching business here in Manhattan?"

"Actually, no. I'm on tour with a rodeo circuit right now."

"What! So you're, like, a real cowboy?" Her mouth dropped open in an incredibly charming way as she studied him as if she'd just met one of her author celebrities. Then she took a long drink.

"I am a cowboy, ma'am. Born and bred." He dipped his head as though he was wearing his hat, and her eyes just widened further.

"And you know how to dance to this music?"

"Yes, I do. In fact, I'd be happy to take you out on the floor."

Her head was nodding before he finished the sentence, so he stood and offered her his hand.

She came barely up to his shoulder, and that could be fun if she was game to try some lifts. He reached for her hands and found she followed him really well. She laughed and jumped and skipped and did whatever he did. Then he reached his hands around her waist and tossed her up.

She screamed but was laughing when he caught her. Her face full of a happiness he didn't often see outside of his family. The song ended, and they clapped and then he motioned back to their food.

"Oh yes!" She hurried back.

With the first bite of hamburger, he groaned in happiness. "This is so good. I'm starving."

"Me too, but I didn't realize it until now." She put some of the sweet potato fries in her mouth.

"Are those even good?" he asked.

She looked down at her fries. "They're amazing. Have you never had them?"

"No. Everyone talks about them being so good, but I don't agree with that vegetable."

Her laugh carried out into the air around them. "What do you mean, you don't agree with it?"

"Well, is it a veggie or a potato? That's two different things right there."

Kate's slow nod told him she wasn't totally following.

"It doesn't matter. Besides, it's orange. I just can't see myself appreciating a potato masquerading about as a vegetable as bright orange as that."

"Well, you'll never know until you try." She held out a long, thick fry, and he knew he'd talked himself right into this mess.

He considered her a moment and then, in a completely uncharacteristic move, FaceTimed his mother.

She got on right away. "Where are you?" Her close-up face on his screen made him laugh.

"Hey, Mama. I'm here at a restaurant with a pretty lady named Kate." He moved the phone so his mama could see her. She waved, seeming perfectly comfortable. He'd known she would be. There was something about her that screamed Willow Creek.

"And Kate here has me convinced I need to try a sweet potato fry."

"No! Bless that woman with all that's good."

"Truly. And so I thought you'd want to witness."

"Oh, you know I do. Bailey, honey, you're not gonna believe. Dylan's gonna eat a sweet potato fry."

Bailey's face showed up next to his mama's.

He tilted the phone so that Kate was back in frame.

"Who's with you? Who's working this magic?"

"As if I can't be tryin' a fraud-like food on my own?"

Bailey waited.

"This is Kate."

Kate waved again, and then he picked up the fry. "Is it better with ketchup?"

"Now, that depends." Kate surprised him by seizing back the conversation. "What say you, ladies?"

"I say no ketchup." Mama placed her vote.

"And I say drown the thing in it. But I drown most everything in ketchup." Bailey shared the phone with his mama.

Dylan turned to Kate. "What say you? You're the tiebreaker."

"I am a purist." She put another fry in her mouth. "Naked is the way to go."

The squeals on the phone made him and Kate laugh. Then he lifted the fry and, with a lot of wiggling and drama, placed it in his mouth. After chewing for a second, he nodded. "Now that ain't half bad. I wish someone would have told me how good it was long before now…"

Their loud responses made him laugh, and he winked and hung up the phone.

Kate watched him. "So that was your mama and…sister?"

"Sister-in-law, yes." He drank several gulps to clear his mouth.

"You didn't really like it?"

"No, it was good. It was. But I think…" He wiped his mouth. "I think I'll stick to regular fries."

They worked on their food, side by side, and by the end of the meal, Dylan was convinced that New Yorkers were nothing like Decker had said. In fact, he enjoyed this particular New Yorker's company quite a lot.

CHAPTER 4

*K*ate couldn't believe her amazing luck. She and Dylan had chemistry. She could feel it. Or was she imagining it? But he looked at her with such an appreciation, he studied her face, he listened. Surely all those things meant he was interested? It had been too long. She just didn't know.

So, while they lingered over their last few fries and refills on drinks, she asked, "How long are you gonna be here?"

"Right. That's what I'm trying to figure out. I don't think I told you. So, I just finished a rodeo across the water in Jersey. And I came up for the weekend."

She nodded.

He shifted in his seat and seemed reluctant at first but then leaned forward with a new excitement. "Maybe you can help me."

"What? Sure, I'd love to."

"Well, I have this girl."

All the energy drained from Kate's face. Of course he had a girl. She nodded, trying to look enthusiastic.

"And, well, I'm here to do one of those gestures."

"Gesture?"

"Sure. You know, it's in all the romance movies, books too maybe, where the guy and girl separate and then he has to prove himself to her so he can at last win her over."

Kate tried so hard to hide her disappointment. She cleared her throat, took another drink, and then nodded. "Okay, so what do you have in mind?"

"Well, I don't know. In fact, I'm not sure she's even happy I'm here. But I had to come. I have to find out. We've been together for a long time. You don't just throw something like that away because one of you moves."

"Are you thinking about moving here for her?"

He seemed unsure. But he nodded. "I am."

"And you need ideas?"

"Yes. And from someone who knows the area. What's romantic? What would make her know I'm serious and willing to do what it takes?"

Who was this man? Why, oh why didn't Kate have some amazing man like Dylan offering to perform a grand gesture to prove his love for her? Was he for real? She shook her head.

"What? Is this a bad idea?"

"Oh, no. I'm wondering why the grand gesture thing is needed in the first place."

"What do you mean?"

"Well, what's wrong with this girl? How could she not know what she has already?" She almost looked away and changed the subject, but something in his eyes, a spark, told her to pause.

"You're real special, you know that, Kate? I'm so happy I ran into you today."

"Me too." Her voice sounded small to her ears. Then she sat up taller. "But now we've got to plan." She dug a notebook out of her purse.

"What, you carry that thing around with you?"

She looked it over. "Of course. Don't you have…" She looked

him over and couldn't help enjoying the slow perusal. "Yeah, I guess you don't have any notebooks on you." She laughed.

"So anyway, let's make a list. All the romantic things to do in New York."

She clicked her pencil and placed it on the paper. "How long has she been here?"

"Just over a year."

"Okay, so she's already seen all the touristy stuff, I'm sure."

"Oh, you're right. So, Empire State Building is out."

"Definitely. That thing takes all day." She rallied herself and made a huge list of fun, offbeat things to do on a date in New York. She even gave him a few of her own favorite places. Then she sighed.

"What?"

"Oh, nothing. Did I sigh?"

"Yes, kind of loud, too. Maybe it's getting late? I'm so sorry to keep you at this when you were probably just here for dinner."

He moved to stand, but she put her hand on his arm. "No, stay. I was just looking at this list and wondering how I could get myself a date to do some of this." She laughed.

"Well, why can't you? Let's talk about that for a minute." He took her notebook, moved to the next blank page, and put his pen to paper. "Who do you know?"

She thought frantically for a name, any name. "There's Javier at work. He's single." Her voice trailed off when he shook his head.

"No. Being single is not enough criteria to want to spend time with this person."

"I give you that, but it is important."

"True. Okay." He wrote down Javier's name.

"There might be someone in my apartment complex." She shrugged . "Honestly, I don't usually get out much. I need to meet some more people."

"Like tonight. You were great at meeting me. You could do that more often maybe?"

"Yeah, like tonight. Except it would help if the guy was available."

The apology in his eyes was sincere. "Most of the time, I bet he will be. And, hey, you were easy to talk to, our dance was amazing."

The music started up again. And he held out his hand. "Let's dance."

She nodded. "You're on."

He pulled her closer this time, or was it her imagination? They did a two-step kind of waltz, and even though she'd never really danced country, he made it so easy. He took her all over the room, and they spun, and he dipped her, and by the end she was laughing harder than she'd laughed in a long time.

Then the music slowed. She made a move to go sit, but he pulled her back into his arms. "I'd like to thank you for tonight, Kate."

"Oh, thank you. Honestly, it was just what I needed." She didn't tell him she'd been kept awake with thoughts of an imaginary cowboy just like him. "It's been a long time since I've had this much fun."

He began to move slowly around the room with her in his arms. "What are your goals? Do you want to stay with this agency?"

"I think so." She pressed her lips together. "Or perhaps a position will open in a publishing house. I like the editing side of things almost as much as the selling."

"Well, I wish you the best."

"Thank you. And you? Are you going to ride in rodeos forever?"

He shook his head. "No. In fact I just got the chance of a lifetime, a career-making opportunity, and I just can't feel that excited about it."

"Why not?"

He shrugged. "Other things just seem to matter more." He looked into her eyes. "You know, Kate, you can meet all kinds of guys in a bar like this. You be real careful when you do this again."

"What do you mean?"

"Well, like letting him hold you and dancing and buying you dinner. A guy could be any number of things." She nodded, not sure where he was going with the conversation. "I'm just saying, be careful."

"Thank you."

"In fact, can I have your number?"

She opened her mouth in surprise for a half second and then choked out, " Sure."

"Good. I'll text you so you know how to reach me. If you need anything while I'm here, you just reach out."

"And if you want some more help with your grand gesture, I'll do my best."

"Thank you. I just might need some help. What if I did candles and roses and things? I'm pathetic at all that stuff women want."

"That's not the stuff that matters."

They didn't say much else while they danced. When the music ended, he held her a moment longer before leading her back to their table. "I think it's about time I call it a night. Can I walk you somewhere?"

"No, I'm just right across the street."

"Me too."

They walked out together and waited at the light. "I heard this hotel was one of the best. But I'm just staying there because it's right next door to Shelby."

"Shelby!" Kate's heart dropped to her toes.

"Wait. You know her?"

"She's my roommate!" She wanted to bury her face in her hands.

"So I'll see you again!" His happiness was so genuine she felt a bit of warmth along with the disquiet that upset her peace. This man, this gem of a human, was the one caught up in Shelby's web?

She opened her mouth to say something, anything, but the light changed and they began to walk across the street. "How lucky that the first person I meet in New York is Shelby's roommate. What are the odds?"

"Totally."

They walked in quiet a moment.

"You're not saying much." He studied the side of her face because she wouldn't turn to look at him. She couldn't. Not yet. Lest she blurt out all the negative things she knew about Shelby. This man? With Shelby? She couldn't see it, not for anything.

"How long have you two dated?"

"All of high school. I've known her since she was like ten. Though back then I didn't like her one bit. She was that girl in school that only ever talked about herself."

Kate nodded. She'd seen no difference in her adult self. "And how did you leave things?"

"Well, she broke up with me." He seemed to hesitate. "But I do hope it's one of those situations where the woman breaks it off but she's missed me and will appreciate if I make the first move." The expression he turned to her was hopeful.

But she shook her head. "I don't know. I will do my best. But she hasn't talked about you much." Or at all, she thought.

"Excellent."

When they were standing in front of her apartment building, she indicated the intercom. "Just push this button here. It rings our apartment and we can open the door from there."

"I will. Now, can I get that number?"

"Oh, right."

"It's even more important now. Though, I guess I'll see you in the morning."

She gave a half nod then a full. "I work from home. Will you be coming up?"

"We're going to breakfast. I think I'll try the Waffle Maker place you suggested."

Kate shook her head, irritated with herself for being in this position. "No, not for Shelby."

"I thought you said it was scrumptious." He pulled out the paper. "See, right here."

"Right. For me." And most people. "It is delicious. But she's worried about carbs. She might like the Red Onion."

"The Red Onion?"

"Yeah. It's her regular stop. Has all vegetables and eggs and smoothies with no dairy. That kind of stuff."

He considered her a moment and then put the paper back in his pocket. "Makes sense. She always was careful with what she ate."

"But if you want to try out Waffle Maker, I'd be happy to go when she's busy." Had she just said that? The words tumbled out without a plan. Was she trying to get in with Shelby's boyfriend? Ex-boyfriend, she reminded herself. And after a moment's thought she knew she wasn't. She just saw how badly he wanted to do waffles. And she loved the place, so why not? Besides, hadn't Shelby told her to keep an eye on him and entertain him when she could?

Conscience comforted, she reached for the door. "Thanks for tonight, Dylan. I'll see you in the morning."

"Right. Thanks." He stood, watching her until the door closed behind her. Then she puffed out every breath of air in her body, feeling herself deflate into an imaginary heap. "What am I doing here?"

With one hand at her forehead, ready to nurse a rising

headache, she made her way up the elevator, down the hall, and into her room without collapsing.

But as soon as she'd washed her face and brushed her teeth, she curled into a ball. The very best man she'd met....ever...was being used by her roommate. And he was obviously still so totally into her that he would never want to date anyone else.

With one pillow against her chest, she rolled over onto her side and prayed a little extra that night that she could get some rest.

CHAPTER 5

*D*ylan made his way back up to his hotel room, strangely unsettled.

Why hadn't Kate seemed happy about Shelby? For a brief second, a flash of something had crossed her face. Guilt? Warning? Pity? He mulled it over. He didn't really know Kate at all, certainly not enough to know the nuances of her facial expressions. He smiled. But she was one cool woman. Maybe for someone in his family? Decker? The idea felt great, but foreign. They would hit it off immediately. And why was that wrong?

He didn't want to analyze it. But for now, he didn't want Kate to hit it off with anyone, and he was not necessarily wanting to hit it off with her either. He was there in New York to see if he could make amends with Shelby—to see if him being willing to move would show her that they could be together.

His thoughts broke off, interrupted by memories of his evening dancing with Kate. She was a totally newbie at the whole country dance thing, but she was so game and fun and willing. And not once did she worry about how she looked.

How had she looked? He closed his eyes, trying to remember. He didn't know what she'd been wearing, couldn't imagine how she'd done her hair. She just had this great smile. A few freckles and a dimple. He smiled. That's it. And her eyes. Deep brown. He shrugged.

That's the thing about Shelby. He could close his eyes and see everything. Her latest manicure, the highlights in her hair, the way her teeth sparkled, every new shade of lipstick. He'd once given him a tour of her makeup, and she would switch between shades of lipstick, sometimes asking if he noticed. He laughed. He'd learned really quickly if he wanted to show her he cared, he had to pay attention to all of that. One time he hadn't noticed that her toenails matched her fingernails—and apparently she'd done it for him.

He scratched his head. He could picture Shelby in all her looks.

When he finally turned off the lights, he thought of what he would say to her tomorrow, but the last thought he had right before falling asleep was an odd sense of relief that Kate would be there.

In the morning, he dressed with care in Shelby's favorite color. He put on the cologne she bought him, brushed his teeth three times, and shaved extra carefully. Then he made his way next door to their apartment building. Remembering what Kate had said last night, he pushed the buzzer.

It was Kate's voice that answered. "Hey. Come on up."

The door clicked and he pushed it open. A man sitting behind a desk glanced in his direction but basically ignored him. The place looked nice but smelled like ten-day-old curry. He wrinkled his nose and pushed the elevator button.

They were on the sixth floor, number 6235. That was the number next to their names. Shelby and Kate. That's all it had said. Maybe that was safer, not giving out full names? He didn't know. This whole way of life was so foreign compared to the fields and mountains that surrounded the Dawson land in Willow Creek.

When he stepped out into the hall, Shelby exited the door three doors down. She hadn't seen him yet. She was on the phone. Her face was tighter than he remembered. Maybe she was stressed about something. But she was as beautiful as ever. As soon as she looked up, her face grew into a large and natural smile.

He couldn't help but feel giddy from his head to his toes. If his brothers could see his goofy smile, he was sure he'd hear about it for weeks, but he didn't care. There was Shelby, right in front of him. "Hey, babe." He stepped closer, holding out his hands.

She put her phone in her purse and hugged him back. She was stiff, skinnier than he remembered, and the hug was way too quick. "Dylan! It's good to see you! How's everyone back home?" She wrapped her hands around his arm and led him back toward her apartment.

"Everybody's great. They ask about you."

"Oh, how cute. I'm fine. Tell them that. Tell them hello and that I'm having the time of my life."

"I will. Hey, you look good." She smelled different. He couldn't place it. New shampoo? New perfume? It was nice but not his same Shelby.

"You're wearing the cologne I bought for you."

"Yeah, of course."

"We were so young then. It brings back the mems. But you can wear something else if you want. You don't have to keep smelling like you're in college." She stepped into her apartment.

"Oh, okay." He didn't know quite how to respond to that one.

Their apartment was small but cozy. Three bookshelves full of books lined one wall. He smiled, knowing who's those were.

She must have noticed the direction of his gaze. "My roommate's a literary agent. She's actually read all those, can you believe it?" She wrinkled her nose as if that was slightly distasteful. And he was left with a deflated feeling. Kate hadn't mentioned meeting him.

A door on the other side of their living space opened, and Kate stepped out. Her hair was messy and fell all around her, and she was dressed in what looked like pajamas. She stopped and waved. "Oh, hello." Then she continued on into the kitchen.

Shelby shook her head. "That's Kate." She waved her hand around. "And this is our apartment. Hey, you wanna get going? I have to get to work right after breakfast, but you're welcome to come back here. Kate has some work to finish up, but then she said she'd show you around."

Kate peered around the column between them and smiled and then shrugged.

"Sure. We can talk about it at least."

Kate nodded and opened the refrigerator.

Dylan's world shifted uncomfortably around him. Nothing seemed to be sitting right. But he pasted on a smile and said in an overly cheerful voice. "You ready?"

"Yes, let's go or we'll never beat the crowds. You wouldn't believe the pace we lead here. I'm going and moving and working or going out every hour. It's so much more than Willow Creek has ever been."

Dylan pressed his lips together for a moment and then followed her out the door. "Decker loves New York. He said his internship was awesome. He would love this talk."

She laughed, a grating kind of fake sound. "But not you. Your heart's stuck in Willow Creek. I bet you hope to have your grandbabies living there alongside you in forty years." She said it like it was not a good thing, like his aspirations were somehow low because of it.

"I'm on the national team for rodeo this year."

She stopped and her eyes grew wider. "What! Really! Like you might beat records?"

He shrugged. "I've already beat most of the records. This

team puts me in place to win nationally and then qualify for the Olympics. Kind of like Maverick was doing before he got married."

She sidled up closer. "Ooh. Wow, Dylan that's impressive. Will you be on TV?"

"All my rodeos this year have been televised."

"But on national stations? So we can watch you here?" She looked up into his face, suddenly flirty.

He smiled back. It was nice to see her eyes go dreamy again for a second. "Yep. I'll let you know all the details. This fall, I start training."

She nodded. "Oh! Do you mind if I pick the place?"

"Nope. Take me to the best breakfast in New York, on me."

She laughed, nervous. "Well, this might not be the best, but it certainly avoids the crowds and I'm kind of in a hurry so…"

"Well, okay that too. Thanks for making time to see me."

"You're welcome. It's tough to fit things in with the schedules we keep out here, but you're from home. We have history. It's good to see you, Dylan."

He wasn't certain what she meant by that, but he would take it. She was happy to see him even if just for old times' sake.

CHAPTER 6

*K*ate paced the floor. She'd deliberately not gotten ready before she saw Dylan. Maybe he would be so appalled by her appearance he'd stop looking at her with a smile in his eyes. She was not into her roommate's ex-boyfriend. She was not. She refused for that to be a thing. No. She was going to work hard on her submission inbox until he came back and then tell him that he was welcome to entertain himself for a few more hours and that she could meet him for lunch.

But as soon as he left, she dropped her bagel on her plate and hurried back to take a shower. The extra eyeliner, the tighter fitting sweater, and her nicest shoes had nothing to do with Dylan, or so she tried to pretend. She was a professional and worked better when she dressed like one.

After finally getting into a groove with her work, she got more done than she'd expected in the next couple hours. When she finally looked up to check the time, the door clicked open, and Dylan stepped back in. Shelby waved to her, blew kisses, and then hurried away.

Dylan was left standing alone in her living room. Wow. He

was so much better-looking than she remembered last night. And he smelled like a dream. Lingering wafts of his cologne had tempted her senses while he was gone.

"Hey," she called out to him. "Want to come sit here for a second while I finish up?"

"Sure. But, Kate, you don't have to entertain me. Looks to me like you've got work to do."

"Well, I do." She waited until he joined her. "But having company is not unwelcome." She smiled and his responding relief was so endearing she almost dropped everything to lead him out the door.

But instead, she said, "I have books. I have television. The Wi-Fi is excellent. Do you have a few minutes?"

"Sure."

"Or you can go tour New York without having to wait around for me..." She didn't dare look at him while she waited for his response.

"No, I want to go with you. If you have time."

"Great."

She pretended to be intently reading her screen, but she was counting the seconds until his incredibly distracting, very handsome face was not looking into her own.

"Kate."

When her eyes met his, she sighed. "Hmm?"

"Why didn't you tell Shelby that we'd met?"

"Oh, um. I hadn't seen her."

"We did get home kind of late." He grinned. "Sorry about that."

She didn't tell him that Shelby had gotten home even later and that she had been on a date with her boyfriend. Though, with his eyes melting her core, the words were on the tip of her tongue.

He got up and wandered over to her books. But dang it! That was more distracting than him sitting right next to her. What was he looking at? He picked one up. She wanted to look over his shoulder and see what it was. Then he put it back and walked down the line of her books. She knew every shelf and a basic order of all the books. His fingers lingered on the classic romance. "Jane Austen."

Did he know Jane Austen? Her favorite author's name on his lips did things to Kate, but she managed to keep her voice calm. "Do you like Pride and Prejudice?"

"Yeah, that Darcy is part of the reason I think I need to do a big gesture for Shelby. Though what he did to solve the whole Wickham situation is more than I can obviously do with this little trip to New York, but maybe it will make a difference."

"How was breakfast?" Kate held her breath.

"It was...different."

She exhaled long and slow. If he and Shelby were going to get back together, he had to at least know what he was getting.

"She seemed happy to see me, though."

Kate nodded. "Great." She went back to her work. Talking about Shelby was not nearly as interesting as she thought it might be.

"But something isn't sitting well with me."

She dragged her gaze back up to his face.

"She brought me to the worst hole-in-the-wall. She didn't like the food any more than I did. And she hurried through it, talked only of herself—but nothing that let me know how she's really doing—and then hurried me back up the stairs." He fell onto the couch. "Sorry. I know you have to work and you're not my relationship doctor." The eyes he lifted up, pleading to her, were too much for her to bear.

She stood, laughing. "Oh, you are doing that on purpose."

"What!" He sat forward. "I'm not doing anything."

"Oh, you are. You're crying out for help and then looking at me with these soulful eyes. How can I resist any of this?"

"Resist? Who says you have to?" He wiggled his eyes in such

a daring, carefree way, she almost chose to take him at face value instead of how he meant her to. She was simply the roommate of the woman he wanted to date.

"Alright. Where should we go?"

He pulled out the list she wrote. "How about we tackle some of this?"

"But don't you want to do that with Shelby?"

"Absolutely. If something is phenomenal, I'll see if I can't get her to go back, but I won't have enough time to get through all this unless we start checking off some boxes. Besides"—he grinned even larger—"didn't you say you were hoping to be able to see some of this stuff?"

She nodded. "I did, yes." After one more moment studying his too handsome face, she nodded. "Okay, we have a lot of ground to cover if we're gonna do even part of that."

"I'm ready."

She raced to her bedroom, changed into sensible shoes, grabbed her purse, and put on a jacket. New York was hot in August usually, but nearing the end sometimes it got chilly, and she had no idea where they might go. A part of her wanted to take the ferry out to the Statue of Liberty, or even better, Ellis Island.

As they walked down the hall, he turned off his phone and put it in his pocket. "So, since it's just you and me, can I talk you into Ellis Island?"

She nearly tripped over her feet as she turned to him. "I was just about to say that!"

"Then it's meant to be."

He had no idea how much meeting him was beginning to feel like exactly that—meant to be. Except for the rather obvious fact that he was hoping to get back together with her roommate.

Once they stepped out onto the street, she raised her hand for a taxi. "Let's get ourselves down to the ferry."

In what seemed like a charmed day, the ferry was getting ready to leave when they grabbed their tickets and stepped aboard. "No lines?" He nodded. "This is great."

"I know. I love it."

The place was mostly deserted. They made their way to the side of the boat that would have the best view of the statue and found seats. But after about five seconds, he stood. "No. We have to stand at the rails."

"Oh, totally." She followed him. It had been a long time since she'd appreciated New York through the eyes of someone else.

And seeing Dylan in New York was just such an odd feeling of opposites.

After a few minutes, a young boy approached them. Kate saw him first, and she pointed down to get Dylan's attention.

He nodded to the boy. "How are you?"

"Hey, do you play for the Giants?"

Dylan laughed, but the question sounded perfectly reasonable to Kate. He was tall and broad and much larger than anyone near them.

He shook his head. "Nope. But I do ride horses for the rodeo."

His eyes widened. "You famous?"

"Yes, I am."

The little boy pumped the air and looked back behind him towards some, as yet, invisible friends. "I told you!" Then he turned back to Dylan. "Thank you, sir. I just won me five dollars."

Dylan laughed. "No problem."

He ran away and around to the other side.

"Do you suppose he's just on here playing around?"

"I don't know. It's free."

"I can see how this would have been a fun way to grow up, maybe."

"But you prefer your hometown."

"Yeah, I do. Where are you from?"

"Oh just suburbia. Nothing like this, but also nothing ranchy like what you had. Just a house. A street. Neighbors. A school."

"Sounds nice too."

"It was. I was safe. It was good." She shrugged, for the first time wondering if where someone lived could be as beloved as Dylan's town was to him.

Words blurted out before she even knew where they were coming from. "Do you pray?"

He paused a moment and then turned to her. "I should pray more."

"But you have before? You try to talk to God?"

"Yes, I do. When I was little, Mama wouldn't let us go to sleep without saying our prayers. And we pray over meals. Do you?"

"Most of the time. Do you know what I prayed to God yesterday?"

He turned to her, his hip leaning up against the railing. "What's that?"

"That I could get out more, have some fun." She laughed.

"Look at you now! Did you think then that you'd be riding the ferry with a stranger?"

"No, I did not." She turned to him. They were closer than she'd realized, but she didn't step away. "But you're not a stranger. At least I don't feel that way."

He studied her for a moment. And nodded. "You're right. You know, maybe there's some good reason as to why we met." He grunted. "It couldn't possibly be a coincidence."

"True. And, you know, I don't really believe in those."

"In coincidences?"

"Right. I just think God's more a part of the little things in our lives than we realize."

"I think you're absolutely right."

45

The ferry moved closer to the statue. And for a long moment, Dylan just stared. "You know, she's beautiful."

"She really is."

"What did our ancestors think when they came into the harbor and she welcomed them all with her torch?"

She thought about that for a long time. A comfortable, companionable silence flowed between them as they moved closer.

"I think you're right," he said.

"About what?"

"There are no coincidences."

She nodded.

It look most of the day, but they toured Ellis Island, found Dylan's ancestors' names for his mama, and made their way back to the ferry stop.

Her feet were heavy, and her body craved some food. But she couldn't bring herself to say she was too tired, that she was done.

"Hey, let's go get some really good food."

"Oh, I'm so happy you said that. I'm starving."

He called for a cab and then surprised her by telling the driver to take them up somewhere close to the park on Fifth Avenue. It might break her bank account to eat at one of the restaurants up there, but she never did anything like this ever, so she was pretty sure her budget could handle a splurge.

They exited the cab, and he took her to an entrance with gold-plated filigree and automatic doors.

The room was dim. The music was soft. She immediately felt underdressed, but Dylan put a hand on the small of her back to lead her up the stairs. "They said they had a table for us and that the loft is casual while the ground level is more formal."

"Oh, great."

They were seated in beautiful, understated elegance. The

waiter filled their waters, and she leaned back in her chair. "This is exactly what I need right now."

"I need food right now." He waved his hand.

The waiter immediately returned. "How may I assist?"

"We need something to start before we even order. Can you bring us your most requested appetizer?"

He nodded his head "Certainly. I'll be right back."

Kate smiled. "I've never seen anyone do that."

"What?"

"Just order something without knowing what it is."

"Well, I figure if most of New York orders it, it must be good."

She studied him. "You're such a fun mystery."

He ducked his head. "I have to confess. You're looking at me as if I'm more impressive than I am. I cheated. I happen to know that the two most requested items are a form of asiago cheese fries and sliders."

"You do not."

"Yes, I do. I read it on their website."

She shook her head. "Well, that's even better because I feel like I could eat those appetizers all by myself."

"Not if I eat them first."

CHAPTER 7

*A*t the end of their too short afternoon, Dylan opened the door to her apartment. "And here we are."

"Thank you. It has been the best day."

"Will you get your work done still?"

She waved her hand. "Of course. And besides, everyone needs a day off now and then, right?"

"I think so." He was standing close. He didn't know if she noticed how close, but he certainly did. And he didn't know what to do with his noticing things like this about her. He took a step back. But then that seemed to add to the awkwardness of the moment since no one was talking.

Kate cleared her throat. "I'm happy you could come. So I'll just, um, get my things together." She turned from him, and he wasn't sure if he should leave or…

She turned back abruptly. "Would you like a drink?"

"Oh, yes. I would." He followed her into the kitchen.

Then Shelby walked in. "Oh, there you are." She reached her hand around his waist and gave him a little squeeze.

He nearly jumped. "Bee. Hey. Kate's been showing me all around New York."

"Have you?" She smiled.

Kate opened her mouth to respond, but Shelby wasn't looking at her and Dylan responded first. "Yes. The Statue of Liberty ferry and Ellis Island—"

"What! She took you to all that! The tourist traps?" She clucked. "Well, tonight we'll go somewhere totally eclectic. Someplace only the locals go."

"Are we going out tonight?"

Kate pushed between them. "Excuse me."

"Oh, hey, thanks again for today," he called after her. She just waved a hand over her shoulder. "You're welcome. Your drink is on the counter."

He picked it up and took a sip. "Wow! This is good." Kate's smile from across the room made him happy. "What's in it?"

"Oh, Kate is fantastic at mixing drinks."

He raised an eyebrow.

"Not those kinds of drinks. She's good at the non-alcoholic kinds. She'll make a Dirty Coke, or a berry Sprite or whatever."

He sipped his drink again. "This is amazingly good. I think there's cherry?"

Kate nodded.

"And vanilla?"

She held up a finger.

"And something else I can't pinpoint." He swooshed the liquid around on his tongue.

Then Shelby stepped in front of him, lifting the glass from his hand and placing it on the counter. "Now. I haven't seen you all day. Let's talk for a minute."

"Oh, sure." He reached around her and picked his drink back up. "But I can take this with us, right? Come on, let's sit."

Was it his imagination or was Kate laughing?

Shelby sat close to him, not quite as close as she had before, but close. He reached for her hand. "Tell me about your day."

And so they did what they had done for all those years. She told him every minute detail, and he listened, asking questions.

Kate moved around on the other side of the room. Now and then she would listen in. She didn't look in their direction, but he could tell. She would tense up and be still and then move about again. At last she sat and opened her computer.

"Are you listening to me at all?" Shelby's lower lip jutted out.

"What? Of course I am." He sat forward. "Do you want to go get something to eat? Or go dancing or something?" His eyes flitted in Kate's direction again. He hadn't had that much fun dancing in a long time.

"Aren't you tired? You've been walking all over New York."

"No, I want to be with you. I only have two days and then I'm back on the road."

"Tell me more about you being such a rodeo star. I miss those days, honestly. The Willow Creek Rodeo, sponsored by the Dawson Ranch. Meet the Dawson brothers." She imitated Maverick's announcer voice, and Dylan laughed. "Wow, you do that well!"

"Ha, well, I've seen enough of them. My favorite was when you'd come riding out."

"I'd point, like this." He held out his arm. "I could always find you in the crowd."

"And now you're winning? Like all the time?"

"Yes. It's incredible, but I'm doing really well."

She leaned closer, their shoulders touching now. "Olympics. What if you make it to the Olympics?" Something flashed in her eyes, a greedy sort of interest that felt…different.

Kate sneezed.

He stood. "Shall we?" Something about her fawning over him in front of Kate made him uncomfortable.

"Okay, I guess." She stood to join him and seemed to drag her feet as she followed him out the door.

He turned. "Where should we go?"

"Wherever. I mean, you can't go wrong really anywhere."

"Except the Statue of Liberty?"

"Well, yeah. I mean, that wasn't wrong either. It was just good Kate took you there. She likes that kind of stuff, and the woman never gets out, so it was good for both of you."

"Why doesn't she get out more? She seems like a great person."

"I don't know. She works hard." She shrugged. "I suggest all the time we should double date…" She let her voice trail off, and he didn't pursue it. He didn't want to know, or perhaps he just didn't want to know right then.

"She seemed to me like she could use some fun in her life."

"I know. She's such a deadbeat sometimes, sitting there working on her clients books and things. It's like she is waiting for her personality to grow." She held a hand up to her mouth. "That came out way more rude than I meant it."

Dylan frowned but he didn't say anything more.

They ended up walking aimlessly. Everything about their time together felt so opposite of Kate. With her, they'd had a purpose, a list, and they'd cranked out a lot in a short amount of time, but this felt like doing nothing for the sake of passing the time.

Shelby sighed next to him.

And it felt like Shelby was really not into it.

He glanced down at her. "So, tell me about your work."

She sighed again. "Oh that. Okay, I guess." As she rambled on about work and the breakroom and the boss who asked them to do so much, he wished he hadn't asked. At a break in the conversation, he said, "Tell me something you love about New York." He was waiting for her face to light up, but she just shrugged. "I love everything about New York. It's so much better for me than Willow Creek. I love the variety of people here. Like, I felt like I might die seeing the same people over and over again back home. Here, I never really have to see the same person twice, unless I want to." She waved her hand at all the people all around them. "That's nice."

"But you can't walk by the old diner and wave at Jessie who basically raised us on the side or go grocery shopping and see your old fifth-grade teacher. You can't go see a homecoming game and know almost every person there, or...well, any of it. There's something nice about that too." He reached for her hand, but she shifted so she was just out of reach. It could have been an accident, or it might not have been. "Come on, Shelby, those people love you. Who here in all this crowd would drop everything and help if you needed it?"

"But that's the thing. I might not want to be helped by some of these people."

"The folks back home, though."

She stopped and faced him. "Look, Dylan, I know. Willow Creek is special. It was an amazing place to grow up. But it's not for everyone. And not everyone is a Dawson." She turned from him. "You ready? I think I want to call it a night."

"Oh, sure."

They turned back toward the hotel and apartment, not saying much else. Dylan knew Willow Creek wasn't for everyone, but he didn't like her complaints about good people in a good place. She sounded ungrateful.

But when she said goodbye in front of her building, she was sweet, kissed him on the cheek, and said she was looking forward to breakfast tomorrow.

Instead of turning and going to his room next door, he lingered on the street. People rushed by. It was early yet. He didn't want to be cooped up in that tiny room.

Kate had mentioned a strip of park. It was supposedly well lit at night. He made his way to the High Line and thought about Kate.

He didn't analyze why his thoughts drifted to her, but he couldn't help but compare her and Shelby. He'd had a much better time today with Kate, the roommate. What did that say about his relationship with Shelby?

He didn't really want the answer to that question. Because things had been really good with Shelby in the past. And if they were both willing to make it that way again, they could be really happy. It was tried and tested. They'd made it work for years, and he knew they could do it again. But Kate. He smiled. Were there really people who didn't require so much work in a relationship?

He mulled over that idea for a minute and kind of liked it. But then he walked faster, as if he could leave the thought behind him.

CHAPTER 8

When Shelby picked up her phone and started gushing all over Ramon the minute she walked in the door, Kate couldn't stand to be in the same apartment with her. She'd known Shelby for a year now, had known how she was, and had never felt particularly bothered by it. But now, at this very moment, she felt ill. The air was hot, and she had a sudden urge to be outside.

When Shelby started blowing kisses and promised to be ready in fifteen minutes, Kate couldn't be there another second. She definitely wanted to avoid helping her choose her outfit. Kate grabbed her purse and headed for the door.

"Where are you going?"

Kate turned. Shelby had hung up, and a new suspicion lurked in her eyes.

"Just need some air."

She studied her a moment then nodded. "Maybe we should turn on the AC. It's getting warmer."

"It's getting cooler too. So hard to tell this time of year." Kate hardly heard her own reply, such mundane words.

"What did you think of Dylan?"

Kate held her breath. *Please don't blush.* And then shrugged. "You're right. He's a great guy. Total cowboy." She laughed. "Is that what guys are like where you're from?"

"Pretty much. But..." She pouted. "No one is like Dylan, not really, not even his other three brothers."

Kate's mouth dropped. "There are three more Dawson brothers?"

"He didn't tell you? You spent, like, the whole day together." Did Kate imagine a hint of accusation in her voice? She started to bristle. She'd taken off work and entertained Shelby's ex-boyfriend for her. She didn't need whatever this was.

"I'm behind now, so if you're hoping I'll babysit the cowboy tomorrow, you might want to make other arrangements." She opened the door and stepped out before she could hear Shelby's response.

Where did Shelby think that conversation was gonna go? Was she gonna ask if Kate was attracted to her ex-boyfriend? Accuse her of spending too much time with him? Try to warn her off? Well, Kate had just been doing what Shelby asked her to, and she'd been dumped on unexpectedly for an afternoon date as well. She walked faster. Date. She knew that the reason she was so bothered had a lot to do with the fact that she was totally crushing on him, even though she tried not to be.

Shelby so didn't deserve him, and she didn't have any right to be possessive of him. How could she send any sort of attitude at Kate when she had just gotten off the phone with Ramon? When Kate knew that Dylan had all these hopes to do everything and be everything so that Shelby would take him back

Kate walked faster still, pushed past the reception desk and slammed open the door to outside. Not seeing anything, she blindly pounded the pavement, every step a rebellion against her situation. She finally went out with a guy. The irony being it wasn't even a real date. He was determined to win her roommate's heart. But she did finally go out with someone, and he was probably the best man she would ever date—he was hands down the most appealing. And she also knew that he was so tantalizingly out of reach she would never be able to be with him again.

She shook her head. "No." She was not going to be home when he came tomorrow. She was not going to be around even if Shelby begged. She could take care of her own situation. And Kate would be... She considered. Where would she be? "I will go to the library." She loved the New York Public Library. She'd studied there every day of her four years at NYU. And she could do it again. She'd ask for a room so she could make phone calls. Having a plan calmed her heart somewhat. And she started to notice her surroundings. She was approaching the High Line. She laughed to herself. Of course. She loved to walk along the High Line. It was an elevated park of sorts that went for a long ways through New York City. And especially at this time of day, she loved to walk along and feel the cool breeze.

The nearest entrance was across the street, a red metal staircase. She waited at the light, still feeling the defiance and irritation from earlier, but it waned as she realized that even though she was stubbornly insisting to leave, she really and truly, most desperately wished to see him again.

But why torture herself? Why spend time with someone who would never be hers? Her feet slowed and she now dragged herself up the stairs. She shook her head. And besides, she knew nothing about him. What kind of man fell in love with someone like Shelby? She snorted.

By the time she reached the top, the night opened up to her. The tiniest star twinkled above, and the breeze caressed her skin. Everything started to feel much better. She walked along, planning to keep walking until she felt all the way better.

Couples passed her, holding hands, smiling, and she wondered how she would ever have something like that in her life. It certainly wouldn't happen if she continued on the way she was. It couldn't happen if she never went out or socialized or really even communicated with anyone besides about work.

There had been talk of writing conferences. Maybe she should start there. She could be the one the agency sent to hear pitches and give presentations at conferences. They were always looking for volunteers. Then she would travel at least, meet people. She nodded.

And maybe she could stomach a double date or two with Shelby. Her roommate certainly knew a lot of people. And… She shuddered. And maybe she could join a dating app. Then she laughed at herself. All this change because she met a hot cowboy?

"Kate?"

She stopped, his voice rumbling up through her core. Had she just imagined up Dylan?

"Kate?" He was coming closer.

She turned. "Dylan?" Her smile grew until it filled her face. Her heart leapt in happy expectation, and her traitorous reactions all but obliterated every other sensible thing she had just been thinking. Plans? What were plans?

"What are you doing here?" Kate rocked back and forth from toe to heel, smiling and not even caring that she must look like an overly pleased teenager.

But he seemed just as happy. "I couldn't sleep. I've been walking along this High Line. Great recommendation by the way."

"How long have you been out here?"

"Since I left your apartment." He laughed. "I'm used to space. This is good for me."

"Oh, of course. We should go up to Central Park." We? Had

she just said *we*? Like they were a regular thing. Like she was going to hang out with him tomorrow instead of going to the library. The train wreck that used to be her plans was falling apart around her.

"I think Shelby made plans for tomorrow." He looked away. "Though I'm not sure what."

"Right. Great. That's good. I forgot I really need to work tomorrow, anyway. But if she asks what you want to do, the park is nice. You forget for a minute that you're surrounded by people and buildings." She kind of wanted to hide again. And she certainly wanted to leave him be on the High Line. Why had she told him about it?

"Do you want to sit for a minute?"

"Um. Sure." Did she? Sort of. Like, she totally did want to sit with him, but she knew it was not a great idea. It was one of those things that would give her instant gratification but she would regret later. It was like that marshmallow test with kids. Her mind argued against sitting with Dylan, but she just stepped forward and sat. They faced the lights of New York and, a few blocks away, the water. In between the buildings, they watched boats floating by, full of lights.

"This is nice." Dylan nodded. "You've shown me the best parts of New York."

"I'm glad. I think it's easy to forget all the cool stuff if you're here awhile. Shelby has been here forever." Why was she defending that woman?

"Hmm." He didn't say anything more, and she didn't want to ask what he was thinking. The last thing she wanted to be was a confidante about his relationship with Shelby.

"I just don't understand her, Kate."

She closed her eyes and breathed twice before she turned to him. "What do you mean?"

"Well, she acts happy to see me, but when we're together it's like she's enduring every minute and can't wait to get back to the apartment." He pressed his lips together and then faced her. "Where is she right now?"

Kate hesitated.

"No, never mind. If I want to know, I'll ask her."

Kate breathed out in relief. "Honestly, I don't know."

He nodded.

There. She was clueing him in that Shelby wasn't home without having to be some kind of go-between or snitch.

Though, he deserved to know. Hopefully Shelby would communicate something that let him know he would be better off finding another woman.

Before she could stop herself, the very next thought raced through her, consuming everything else. That next woman. It could be anyone. Why not Kate?

She sank her head into her hands.

"What is it?" He leaned closer beside her so that his cologne cascaded all around her, and she breathed deeply.

"I think I'm just tired."

"Is something bothering you? I took up your whole day and never really considered how much of a burden it could have been on you."

His real concern, his caring eyes, all of it was almost too much.

"I do have a lot of work I need to do, but I always have a lot of work to do. I think I realized today that I need to worry less about work and actually get out and enjoy myself."

He nodded and was quiet for so long that she wasn't sure he was aware of her beside him any longer. Then he said, "I think you're like Decker."

"Decker?"

"My twin."

She choked. "You have a twin?" Her smile grew.

"Now just a minute, what are you so happy about?"

She shook her head in wonder. "Nothing at all. I'm just...I don't know. It's good to know there's someone else like you in the world." As she said the words, she was almost embarrassed by what she was admitting. But it couldn't be helped. Even if he wasn't for her, it gave her hope that there might be another. "I knew there were four of you Dawson brothers. But a twin..."

"As I was saying..." His tone had a hint of irritation to it, but she could sense that he meant nothing by it. "You sound like Decker. He is the one I think might actually move out here and work in one of these buildings. I think he secretly wants to."

She nodded, liking the sound of this twin more and more.

"He's driven and works hard, and when the ranch was struggling and our older brother needed some help, he let it all go and put all his energy into the ranch and building our business."

"That was really great of him to do that."

"Yup. And it's good there are people like him in the world. Someone needs to work in the companies and help publish the books. But even those people need a little bit of beauty in their lives."

She knew he spoke the truth. She'd been feeling the lack of anything beautiful in her life. "I think I'd do better work if, every now and then, I had nights like this one."

He shook his head. "Not every now and then. Every night. Why not? Get out, enjoy where you live."

"Is that what you do?"

He thought about her question for a moment, at least she assumed he was thinking about it. Then he nodded. "I think so. But I gotta tell you, my whole life is kinda like this right now."

"Like sitting here on a bench?"

"Not totally, but lots of sitting and thinking and riding Pepper."

"Pepper?"

"My horse."

She sucked in a breath. She'd not thought too much about the fact that he must have his own horse. "What kind is he?"

"Oh, he's a beaut. The best rodeo horse a guy could ever want. I trained him myself. I can rope anything when I'm up on his back."

"Anything?"

"Yup."

Her smile twitched and he must have noticed.

"You thinking about challenging my claim?" His one eyebrow rose higher up on his forehead.

"Yes, I am actually. I think there are things you could not rope from a horse."

His gaze turned wicked. "Now, Miss Kate, those words are gonna have to be proven wrong, you know that."

"Are they?"

"Yes, and I think you're just gonna have to be present to see your words die an untimely death."

"Where is this Pepper?"

"Well, right now he's in Jersey, but he and I travel all over the country."

"How long are you in Jersey?" Her words sounded more breathless than she would have liked, but he was offering something she could hardly resist. A horse. Him riding a horse, nearby.

"Well, I leave day after tomorrow, but I'll be back, and I'll be in lots of other places. I'm just gonna have to let you know where I'll be, and you name the day and time that your assumptions meet their demise."

She laughed. "Oh, you are too much. This I have to see."

"I hope so." He reached for her phone. "Here, I'll put my number in there. You text me and I will start sending you my schedule."

"This is too good. You are so on."

"I hope so, because now that we've talked about this, I'm

gonna be searching rodeo crowds for your pretty hair and I won't feel satisfied until you're in my audience."

"Is that so?"

"Yes, little lady, that is most definitely so." He tapped her nose, and she realized that without trying at all, they'd fallen into a sort of fun back-and-forth that might almost be considered flirting.

She searched his face. He seemed totally relaxed and comfortable.

"Then we'll make it happen. But I'm gonna be searching out all the different things that would be impossible to rope."

"Have at it. I'm telling you, there's nothing my Pepper can't do."

She smiled as she pocketed her phone. This conversation was definitely too good to be true, but she'd enjoy it while it lasted.

They sat in companionable silence for a moment. His shoulder was just shy of hers, just an inch. If she shifted, they'd be touching. She rested her hand on her lap, knowing he would never take it, but there was a thrill in just being close.

She shook her head.

"What is it?"

"Oh. Nothing really, just thinking about how nice this is." She summoned a bit of courage. "And knowing it won't last." She laughed. "The stars, the nice breeze, New York, the water. It's romantic."

His smile was warm. "And we're not in a romantic place."

"Right."

"Yeah, I see that. But it's still nice. I'm glad I got to know you, Kate."

"Oh? Why's that?"

"It's nice to know someone like you is possible."

She leaned closer to nudge his shoulder with hers. "That's exactly what I thought."

"No coincidences."

"Right."

"I know God sees us. He's involved in all these little details."

She heard the words and felt the magic of this brief snapshot of time. What on earth could God's purpose be with the two of them?

CHAPTER 9

*S*omething about sitting this close to Kate, enjoying the beautiful night, and hearing her faith and encouraging words was unsettling to Dylan. In an almost pleasant way, he felt like he'd just got bucked off a bronco. He needed to get his mind back on track or he might make the mistake of his life and become distracted by Kate right when he finally had a chance with Shelby.

And maybe that was it. God had placed Kate in his life so that she could help him know what to do to win back his girl.

He sighed. "I don't know what to do."

"That sounds deep. About what?"

"Shelby."

"Oh."

"I came all this way. I want to give it my best shot, but I feel like she's making that difficult."

Kate nodded.

"You agree? Is she?"

"Is she what? Making it difficult?"

"Yeah. I don't want to put you in an awkward position, but any tiny bit of help you can give me would be so appreciated."

She studied him for a moment, her face blank. Then with a sort of resigned air, she stood and walked to the railing.

He joined her.

"You need to take charge of the situation."

"What?"

"You're coming in here all hopeful and ready to catch a bone, but you need to take charge. Plan the dates. Make the move. Be a cowboy."

"Be a cowboy?" He laughed.

"Yeah, you know, tall and tough, honorable, strong." Her words took on a wistful sort of sound.

"So, you like cowboys, then?"

Her cheeks colored. But she waved him off. "Never mind me. Do this and you might have a chance."

"Okay, that's easy, but she's just so difficult to pin down."

"Act like you don't know her. How would you try to win her?"

"That's easy too."

She waited, and when her eyebrow rose in challenge, he laughed out loud. "Again with the challenge?"

"I'm seeing a lot of claims coming from your direction. Whaddya got, cowboy?"

He rubbed his hands together. "You are so right. I have one more day. That woman isn't going to know what hit her."

"That's the spirit." Kate smiled.

They talked some more, but his mind was already spinning with ideas to win back Shelby. He was itching to get on his phone and start making some calls, placing some orders, and making some reservations.

As if Kate could sense his attention had shifted, she stepped away from the railing. "Well, I think I'll get back now. It's getting late."

"I'll walk you back. I've got my work cut out for me."

"I can't wait to see what you have up those sleeves." Her gaze lingered on his arms and moved across his chest for a brief moment and then she turned. "Come on."

After he said goodnight to her at the door, he immediately made a couple searches for local florists. "To start, her favorite flower."

Kate was gonna be blown away by this. He stopped. And Shelby too, of course. He laughed at himself. Somehow proving himself to Kate, rising to her challenge, was becoming just as important. Talk about competitive. He shook his head. Kate was a great woman. When she asked about Decker, he knew he should have encouraged that more. She really would fit in perfectly with his family. But he just couldn't bring himself to go there just yet. He had her number. He'd have to get a picture of her so he could show his brother. Maybe.

He made a whole bunch of reservations and a stream of delivery orders and then hopped in the shower, whistling. Things were much better when he had a plan. Kate was absolutely right. Did he know how to win over Shelby? Yes he did.

When he got out of the shower, his phone was blowing up with messages. "What on earth."

He picked it up. *Mama's in the hospital.* Everyone was telling him. Text after text. Decker had texted, "Where are you?" He scrolled through, his heart pounding. When he found the first doctor's prognosis, he fell to the bed in relief. A scare, but a real one. He typed, "I'm here. Just got all your messages. I'll be getting on the earliest flight."

He scrolled through available flights, grabbed one leaving at six in the morning, and then moved to the window. Not really paying attention to the alleyway, he searched upward for a star or two. "God, thank you for taking care of my mama. Please help her to live a long time, at least long enough to meet my wife and children." Kate's beautiful face came into his mind, so like his mama in a lot of ways. He smiled. She really was a good woman, such a help to him this trip. He would miss her.

He whipped out a text while he was thinking about it. "Emergency back home. I'm flying out in the morning. You and Shelby enjoy the day I've planned." He laughed to himself while he sent the itinerary. She was going to be blown away.

Then he lay back on his bed, staring up at his ceiling until he finally drifted off to sleep.

By the time he was back at the Dawson ranch, Mama was home from the hospital. At least that's what his phone was telling him. He payed the Uber driver and hopped out of the car at a run.

Decker met him at the door. He hugged his brother a little bit extra.

"She's fine. She's pale. Be ready for that. But she's gonna be fine."

"What did the doctor say?"

"She's just got to take it easy and be careful what she eats. Blood thinners."

They entered the front room, and Dylan breathed deeply. "I love how it smells at home."

"That? That's just Nash." Maverick joined them and pulled him into a back-pounding hug. "Good to see you, brother."

"You too."

"Come on, let's go show Mama who came back."

Dylan laughed but swallowed the sharpness in his throat. He stepped up to her door. His parents' master bedroom brought back such a longing for his father in this tender moment that he wiped at his eyes with the back of his hand. Decker's hand on his shoulder told him he was feeling it too. Then he entered the place that had always been a safe haven for him growing up, a place to share his troubles, a place where both his parents had helped him work through all kinds of problems.

Mama smiled at him from her bed. "There's my Dylan!" She reached out a hand. "Do you have time for this, honey?"

"Of course I do." He took her hand and leaned down to kiss her head. "How are you feeling, Mama?"

"Oh I'm fine now. We just had a little scare." Her smile was tired, and a slight wobble in her lips tore at him.

He and Decker shared a concerned glance.

"What do you need? Do you have these guys all doing their chores?" Dylan squeezed her hand and held it while he sat at the side of her bed.

"Oh, they're working all right. All of a sudden, the hay's in. The fall crops planted. Even my flower beds are cleared and ready for the mums." She laughed.

"And I smell something delicious coming from the kitchen."

"That'll be our dear Bailey. Bless that woman. She's not left my side through it all."

"She's a blessing to be sure." Dylan again felt a pang for his own loneliness.

"As soon as all you boys find good women, you will know what I'm talking about." She closed her eyes. "They say I won't be so tired in a couple days."

"I'll let you rest now." Dylan stood.

"Thanks for coming, son. I know you're busy, and I appreciate it." She opened tired eyes again, and the love that shone back at him filled some of that loneliness.

"You're welcome, Mama. I'll always come back."

"That's what your father would say. And I do know he comes now and again. I feel so close to him now." Her voice drifted at the end, and he and Decker left quietly and shut the door.

As soon as they were further down the hall, Dylan shook his head. "So, stroke?"

"They think so."

He didn't know what else to say. He'd never seen his mama look so weak. "I'm so happy you're all here."

His phone rang. *Shelby.* "Oh, dang."

"Are you guys talking again?" Decker's voice was deceptively bland.

"Sort of. I was in New York visiting her." He winced and then answered. "Hey, babe. I mean, Bee."

"I expected you an hour ago. If we don't get going, I won't have time to do anything. I have a busy day today."

Her words grated. But he'd forgotten to let her know. It was probably better Kate hadn't been the one to tell her. Why hadn't Kate told her? "Did you get the flowers?"

She sighed. "Yes, of course. I was going to thank you in person, but I've been waiting here forever."

"Sorry, I guess Kate didn't tell you. Something's come up at home. Mama was sick, so I flew back to be with everyone. But Kate has the itinerary for today. I planned all this for you. I hope you two enjoy it. Take pictures."

"So you're not coming at all now?" Her huff was amazingly callous.

He paused before saying what immediately came to mind, which he knew she couldn't appreciate.

"I'm sorry. I'm so sorry. Give your mama a hug from me, will you? Is she okay?"

That sounded more like the Shelby he knew.

"Hey, thanks. It's rough. She's doing well, though. Home from the hospital and healing."

"That's a relief. Keep me posted if anything comes up."

"I will. Thank you."

"You're welcome."

The pause that followed felt thick and suddenly awkward. He would have said *I love you*. It felt like a good place to say it, given the circumstances and their history, but the words wouldn't form. Not on her end either, apparently.

"Well, goodbye. Enjoy your day."

"Thank you."

When he hung up, Decker was watching him. But he just shook his head.

"You hoping for something there?" Decker asked.

"You know I always have been."

"And now?"

Dylan ran a hand through his hair. "I think I just lost my opportunity." He turned to his brother. "But that might not be all that bad. Maybe."

They entered the living room, and Grace ran at him with a huge hug.

"Hey, Gracie! You've grown! Let me see you." He stood back and measured her up against him. "Yes, definitely taller."

She shrugged. "That's what everyone says every time they see me."

"Oh, well let's talk about something much more interesting, then. I hear you got another dog."

"Yes!" She whistled and three large dogs came running.

"Not in the house!" Bailey stepped out into the living room. Maverick's wife looked round with child and, in Dylan's mind, beautiful because of it.

"Bailey, good to see you."

After a kiss on the cheek, Bailey pointed at the door, and Grace led her dogs outside.

Dylan followed. "How about you show me just how smart these guys are."

"Okay! They're not as smart as the pigs, honestly, but I've got them doing tricks."

Bailey participated in the Dawson 4-H program and pretty much spent all her time as a rancher, or so he'd heard. Once summer was over, she'd be heading back to school with much grumbling.

Decker watched all her dogs' tricks and then helped Maverick with some of the horses and dug into unloading some hay bales. By the time he'd spent a full day on the ranch, something important clicked back into place in his mind. For the first time since Shelby had broken up with him, he felt okay alone. He was happy about it.

He was never really alone, not with a family like his. And watching them all come together for Mama proved to him once again just how close they all were.

CHAPTER 10

*K*ate blinked twice, trying to understand what she was seeing.

Shelby stood in her doorway, super bright light spilling in around her. Hands on hips, her roommate did not look pleased. "Why didn't you tell me that Dylan wasn't coming today?"

"What?" She checked her watch and then sat up. "Is that the time?"

"Yes. Of course it's the time. Now, could you please explain this." She opened up Kate's door wide.

A room full of lilies met her gaze. Kate sucked in a breath. "That's beautiful." She climbed out of bed and tiptoed out into the apartment reverently.

Shelby brushed by them all. "How am I going to explain this to Ramon?"

Kate breathed in the delicious smell and then snapped a few pictures. "This is incredible. Did he send a card?"

"Yes." Shelby waved a hand toward the kitchen table.

His note was perfect. "To prove myself." She laughed out loud.

"What is so funny?"

"This note. I don't know. Don't you think it's funny?"

"There's more on the back."

"And to Shelby. Babe, we can make this work."

Kate tapped the card, secretly enjoying that this huge display was partly for her. Even if for unromantic reasons, she appreciated every single one of those flowers. "Stand next to them." She held up her phone.

"What? No!" She patted her hair.

"Oh please, you look beautiful. This is to let him know you got them."

"You guys text now?"

Kate shrugged. "I don't know. I think he'd appreciate it."

She pouted, and Kate took the picture. Shelby shook her head. "Why do I feel like I'm missing something?"

Because you are. A really awesome guy was doing everything he could to win her heart. "We better get showered up. Our first appointment is in two hours."

"Appointment? What appointment?"

"From Dylan. I guess he's planned a whole day for you." Kate turned and closed her door. She hoped he was okay. She didn't know what the emergency was. But she would set aside work again and go through this day for him. She smiled. And she suspected she'd enjoy it a great deal.

They left together, Kate more cheerful than she'd been in a long time, oddly, and Shelby more frustrated. "I just don't understand why he'd tell you all of this. You knew he was gone. Why didn't he just tell me?" Her pout jutted out more than usual.

But Kate just shrugged. "Sometimes men like to have surprises?"

She seemed partially appeased by that answer. In truth, Kate didn't know, but she was pleased she could be there for him in a moment of great distress and that he'd thought immediately to tell her. That meant something.

After a morning full of one amazing stop after another, including Serendipity's frozen hot chocolate, mani-pedis off Fifth Avenue, and a tour of an interesting women in wartime museum. Kate smiled at the next reservation. "And now we're doing the full hour-long tour of Central Park by carriage." She almost laughed in glee as this particular reservation was surely motivated solely by Kate.

Shelby rolled her eyes. "Could we just say we did it?"

"I'm supposed to take pictures of each one."

She checked her watch. "But I hate the park, and I really need to get back for my date with Ramon."

"But there are dinner plans, there's a lot more to this day." Kate began to worry Shelby would back out, and she wanted to send Dylan the best news she could since she didn't know what he was dealing with. She'd almost sent him a jillion texts to ask if he was okay, but then she'd delete them before hitting send.

Shelby checked her watch again. "Maybe you could just finish them out for me?"

"What? By myself?"

"Totally. Since you're the one who wants me to do this so bad." She narrowed her eyes, but only slightly.

"Or...we could just tell Dylan we couldn't finish the rest." She knew she'd be doing every single thing Dylan set up out of respect for him and what he might be going through, but she hoped for his sake that Shelby would join her.

"Yes, let's do that. You tell him."

"No way. You tell him. You're the one backing out. This is all for you."

Shelby hesitated, and then her phone dinged. "Nope. That's Ramon. I'm going back to the apartment. Oh, and for the record, those lilies are for you if anyone asks." She turned on her heels and walked five steps before calling over her shoulder. "You coming?"

Kate hesitated and then groaned. "No. I'll go ride the carriage."

Shelby laughed. "I knew I could count on you. Thank you!" She blew a kiss and then hopped in a cab she'd waved down.

Kate was left on the curb on Fifth Avenue facing the direction of Central Park with about five long blocks to walk from where she stood. But the air was cool. The day was beautiful. And she hadn't really spent enough time outside, so she started walking toward the park.

And then her phone rang. *Dylan!* She held her breath for another ring and then answered. "Hello!"

"Kate? You sound out of breath, you okay?"

She laughed. "Dylan! How are you? Everyone okay where you are? I've been worried." *Goodness, let the man answer before you ask him a million questions.*

"Yes, I'm good. Mama had a scare, but she's home and recovering. Thank you. Uh, can you talk? How's the day going?"

She decided she was done covering for her roommate. But she didn't want to make him sad. "I can talk. It's been amazing. Everything has been perfect."

"And now?" She could hear the smile in his voice.

"And now, we're going to the park!" She squealed a little bit as she skipped. "And there will be horses."

"That's what I thought you would do." The smile in his voice made her laugh.

"How could you possibly know I would squeal and skip? Have you ever seen me do such a thing?"

"No. But I knew you had it in you. Now tell me. How did Shelby react?" The hope in his voice made her die a little bit inside. And she bit her tongue on every snarky thing she wanted to say.

"She was amazed. The apartment looks and smells amazing. It looks...like a florist's, but even better. It's like a tropical garden in there. And the mani-pedi, that was probably the best move."

"Not the frozen hot chocolate?"

"Well that too, of course. You know, I feel a little guilty getting to enjoy all this in your place. But I'm not complaining."

"And the horses?"

She paused.

"What? Is she still there?"

"No, Dylan. I'm sorry. She left."

He hummed for a minute. "You know what? That's okay. I'm glad someone is going to get to enjoy them. And probably the most appropriate person. Tell me. Did you smile when you saw it on the list?"

"You know I did. I'm almost there now."

"And you only have to walk five blocks, right?"

"Right. You really planned this so well, it's as if you had a New Yorker helping you out."

"No, no. Hey now, I did this on my own. And now I want to hear it, do I not rock at this?"

She bit her tongue, not sure what to say, and then gave up trying to be clever. "Yes, you blew it out of the park."

"And the rest of the night. Is Shelby out for that too?"

"I don't think so. She had something right now, but I think she's hooking back up with me for the Yankees game."

"Well, thanks, Kate. I sat down here after the best and worst sort of day, and all I wanted to do was talk to you. Thanks for being here and doing this for me. Sounds like Shelby's not totally convinced yet. But..." His voice trailed off.

"But?"

"Well, I think I'm finally okay with that. If she can't see what we could make together, then I think I'm finally ready to move on."

"I'm proud of you, Dylan."

"Thank you. You're a big part of that."

Her hope rose powerfully with each mad pump of her heart. "I-I am?"

"Of course. I thought, if I can enjoy another woman like Kate, I'm ready to move on. I'll know better how to grab onto the one when I see her."

Her hope fizzled out like a small leak in a balloon. It wasn't totally shattered, but she suspected that one day it might be. "Well..." She fake laughed best she could. "Glad I could help."

"Me too. Enjoy your day, Kate. You deserve it."

"Thanks. I'm almost to the horses, so I'll take some pictures and, I guess, talk to you later?"

"Sure. Keep me posted on the whole rest of the night."

"I will."

She clicked off and took a moment to wallow in the disappointment, but she couldn't stay for long because she had always wanted to do this terribly touristy thing and take the full tour through the park in a horse-drawn carriage. She planned to enjoy every second.

CHAPTER 11

*D*ylan scrolled through the images Kate sent from his planned day for him and Shelby. He laughed at the pics of their fingers and toes from the nail salon. Shelby's were pink and Kate's were red. He nodded. Seemed about right. He pulled up the one with Kate standing next to her poor and decrepit-looking carriage horse as if it was the coolest thing in the world. He zoomed in on her face. Her smile was so big and full, her eyes lit. She really was something special. And. He tapped his fingers. That woman needed to get up on a horse, a real one. His phone dinged.

"I bow to your awesomeness." Dylan laughed when he read Kate's text.

He responded, "As you should."

"This was one of the best days of my life, and I was just a tagalong."

"Looks like you were the main attraction for the evening activities."

"True, and I did try to pick up my waiter, but alas, alone."

He laughed. His German Shepherd, Sam, perked up his ears. Kate had gone to his planned and paid-for activities for him.

Even when Shelby wouldn't go. Or couldn't go. He wasn't sure yet why she'd not made an appearance. But Kate had gone. She was one classy lady.

With Sam pressed up against him as he leaned back against the headboard on his bed, he thought about what he wanted to say to Kate. "Thanks." It was so much more than that, but what could he say? "Thank you for helping me not feel like a total loser." He frowned.

His phone dinged again. "You made your point. You can win over the ladies, but that doesn't tell me anything about your roping abilities."

"You would throw that down right now!"

"When can I come see you ride?"

He tapped his fingers on his thigh. Did he want her to come? Of course. She was awesome. She made him laugh. She listened to him. She loved everything to do with a rodeo, at least in theory. She would be a hoot as he showed her all the different animals and explained the events. He grinned. And he could show off a little bit. She was still under the impression that there was something out there he couldn't rope while riding Pepper. He smirked.

"I'm dying to prove you wrong, woman."

"You just cinched it. I'm buying tickets right now."

"Excellent."

His grin hurt his face. "See you in Mesquite."

A couple weeks went by, with him and Kate texting now and then, sometimes she'd send a picture of the High Line bench where they sat, or he'd send Pepper pictures. She seemed to love those. Dylan was back on the road. He had one more show until he'd settle in closer to home, which made him happy. His new national team was using an old fairground outside of San Antonio to practice. He felt glad to be a part of the team, happy to have their sponsors and a coach to help him get ready. Happy to be closer to home. But he'd heard nothing from Shelby. It was as if his short weekend in New York had done nothing to bring them closer together. He had to ask himself, did he care anymore? Additional sponsors were talking to him, and just yesterday, he'd received a call from the best, most renowned US Olympic coach.

As he reached his rodeo dreams, he realized he wanted someone by his side. In his mind, that someone had always been Shelby. He knew how to make it work between them. His phone calls home always left him wanting more of that for himself. Everything was going right, and yet, it felt incomplete.

His phone dinged. *Kate.* He smiled. At least he'd gotten to know Kate.

"I'm coming. And I have a few things I know you can't rope."

"Bring. It. On." He laughed. "Text me when you get here." This last rodeo was in Mesquite, Texas, not exactly close to New York, but she said she had time in between projects.

What were they? He and Kate. He shrugged. He didn't want to know, not yet. She was an awesome friend. And she had a tie to Shelby. That, in and of itself, made things complicated. But he wasn't going to worry about it. This weekend was all about showing off a little and showing a good woman what he loved to do. That's all.

Dylan drove to pick her up at the airport. He'd arranged for her to have the use of a trailer to sleep in if she wanted, or of course she could stay in a hotel, but she'd jumped at the chance to take the trailer.

He leaned up against his car, waiting for her to exit the airport. When her hair finally appeared, bobbing among the others who were piling out of the airport, he stood. Energy coursed through him, but he didn't know what to do with it. So he leaned back against the car, trying to appear relaxed even if he couldn't feel that way.

As soon as she stood in front of him, he stepped forward and then awkwardly stepped back. Should they hug?

Her eyes smiled up at him. Her whole expression was warm and...friendly. Of course they could hug. He pulled her close. Every receptor went into hyperdrive in reaction to her sleek form in his arms. Then he stepped back, "Good to see you, Kate."

"You too."

He reached for her bag, opened her door, and was somehow able to put her overnight suitcase in the trunk and get in the driver's seat without fumbling. He suddenly realized that even though he really liked the idea of Kate coming, he didn't know her that well. He didn't know her as well as Shelby. What would they even talk about?

But as soon as he got in the car, Kate held up her phone. "I have a list."

"A list?"

"Yep. You know how you had one when you came to New York?"

It had been a win-Shelby-back list, but yeah, he remembered.

"Well, I have been wanting to see horses and the animals and all the events for a long time. So I made a list."

"I'll do my best to check off every item, then."

She sat back, a look of contentment filling her face. "Texas."

"Hm?"

"I knew I would like Texas."

He laughed. "We have about an hour to drive. Take a look around north Dallas. You're not gonna see many horses."

"But we will in Mesquite."

"Oh, yeah. You're gonna love this." He winked.

She seemed to settle in perfectly comfortably in his passenger seat. And he realized another thing he appreciated about her. She was totally chill. She just took life as it came and seemed to roll with it in a remarkable way. "We will have about three hours to give you the fastest, most epic tour before I need to get ready for the rodeo."

"Sounds great to me. I'm just here to soak it all in." She dug in her backpack and pulled out a thick, hard-bound book with lots of slips of paper poking out the top. It fell open in her lap as though well-read.

"What's this?"

"This?" Her smile seemed kind of shy for a moment, and he wondered if she was about to share something really special. "I've had this forever. It's just a book of horses." She opened it and started flipping through pages.

He was driving, but he caught some of them. "Hey, you have Pepper in there."

"I do? Which one?"

"The paint. The horse with the large brown splotches." He laughed. "That's Pepper, right there."

"Oh, I love paints." She ran a finger down the page.

"Pepper's a lighter brown."

They talked of horses and breeds and training and bits and bridles until Dylan started to feel like he was training a new rodeo hand. "Wow, you are really into this stuff."

"I am." She shrugged. "I was never able to do more than take some lessons as a kid, but I've always wanted to be involved."

"No 4-H where you were?"

She shook her head. "If there was, I didn't know about it. It wasn't a thing at school."

"And that's a crying shame. You should see my niece train her piglets." He laughed, thinking of Grace. "It's really something."

"I'd like that."

"Really?" He turned to her for a second. "You'd like to see my niece train her pigs for 4-H?"

"Yeah, but I can understand if that's weird or whatever." She looked away and he regretted his incredulous tone.

"No, no. It's not weird at all. It's just that Shelby shied away from this kind of stuff. It doesn't smell pretty." He searched her face in between watching the road, unsure where to take the conversation.

"Oh." Her laugh was a bit nervous. "Well, Shelby and I are different. Is it not something that women usually get interested in?"

"No, no, it's not that either. Wow, not at all. Mama'd be the first to tell you no way. Ranching is hard work and some of us just learn to appreciate the smell." He breathed deeply. "Smells like home and the animals we love and the good work the Lord lets us do every day."

He slowed because they would soon be arriving. He took them down a long, dusty gravel road. "I didn't mean to make you feel anything. I really respect that you're interested in all this. Really, you remind me of my mama."

She grimaced. "Thank you. I know you really respect her."

"Right. That came out funny. You're not motherly or anything." He stopped talking. Why were his words coming out all wrong? He just didn't know what to do with a woman that really and truly liked the things he was passionate about. He'd never had that in his life. Maybe he should have dated someone besides Shelby once. It shouldn't surprise him that there were women in the world that would enjoy ranching. Or horses. Most women liked horses, didn't they?

He pulled into his usual spot, next to a row of trailers. "Okay, I've asked for use of the guest trailer. That's yours right there on the end." He stopped the words that almost came out, *next to mine*.

"Do you want to drop off your stuff and freshen up a bit and meet me right out here?"

"Sure. That's great."

He followed her to the trailer and opened her door. "It's not the Waldorf."

"Thank heavens for that." She stepped up inside. "I've always wanted to stay in one of these. I begged for one of those cross-country road trips as a kid."

He shook his head. "You're something."

"Well, something or not, I'm me. And I'm looking forward to proving you wrong this weekend."

"Oh, are you now!"

"Yes! You know I didn't forget. If you back out, I'll view it as an admission of weakness."

He laughed. "Did you bring closed-toe shoes?"

She looked down at her strappy sandals. "Yes, I did."

"Excellent. 'Cause I'm gonna put you up on a horse."

Her eyes widened in pleasure. A look he was determined to encourage again. And then he closed the door to her trailer.

He washed up a bit in his own trailer and stepped outside right when she did. "You ready?"

"Oh, I'm ready!"

He whistled and Sam came running.

"Is this Sam?" She reached down, and his dog melted at her feet.

She pet his stomach while he groveled in submission.

"Wow, he calls himself a guard dog?"

"What? Sam? Nah. Who's a good boy?"

Sam's tail wagged like crazy.

Dylan shook his head. "Okay, enough of that. Sam can get all the love he wants tonight at the fire."

She nodded and stood again. "Where to, cowboy?" Her eyes looked him over in a way that made him want to stand taller.

"Is that a good thing?" he asked.

"What?"

"Cowboy?" He tipped his hat.

"Well, you did put on your hat." She grinned. "And I guess it depends on who's saying it."

"Folks around here won't recognize me without my hat." He

studied her a moment. "Is it a good thing when you're saying it?"

Her victorious laugh made him smile. "You're really something, aren't you?" She stepped closer. "To me, being a cowboy is the very best way to be."

"All right then." He nodded. "Let's show you what cowboys actually do, and then you can revise that statement if you like."

"Why would I?" Her nose wrinkled in a highly attractive confusion.

"Cause it just isn't that glamorous. But come on, you'll see."

CHAPTER 12

*K*ate didn't know how to explain that the very fact that cowboys were not glamorous added to their appeal. To his appeal. She breathed deeply. Her smile grew.

"Like that smell, do you?" His amused and pleased expression made her laugh.

"I do, actually. It's sort of barn, hay, and Dylan cologne all in one."

"Whoa, now. I did wash up, and so I'm not sure I want my cologne mixed in with the barn smell."

"Too late." He would never know how unbelievably sexy she thought it was. Laughing at her own thoughts, she stepped closer. "It's all I'll think of whenever I smell this cologne." She pretended to take a deep smell of him while leaning in real close. Her feet tripped up while she wasn't paying attention where she was walking, and she almost fell at his feet.

He reached out to steady her. His large, strong hands gently setting her right. She stood taller, sort of wishing that hadn't happened, but sort of glad it did. His palms ran down her arms briefly as he set her right, and she could only wish to lean into him all over again.

"Thank you." She couldn't make a joke of her clumsiness. He stood agonizingly close, the smell he had been mocking filled the air around them. The very air seemed to draw her closer to him.

After a moment of charged nearness, and with a new intensity in his face, he just clucked and tipped his head for a moment. "Watch yourself now, these aren't New York sidewalks."

They kept walking as if nothing was different, but Kate thought her heart would never behave as it should again. She tried to catch her breath. And she began to feel silly. Silly for coming out to see him when they weren't anything. Silly for being so schoolgirl infatuated with the man. Just because he was all cowboyed up didn't mean he was any less in love with her roommate or any more the kind of man she wanted to be with.

Trying to rally some of their earlier normalcy and to put the pressure off of any romantic expectations, she created some space between them. "Tell me about your events. What am I going to see from you today?"

"Come on in here. I'll show you." He led her into the smaller of two barns. "These here are the prize stars of the show." He approached a larger stall with calves. They ran in circles, bumping into each other.

"They're cute. How can you tie them up?"

"They don't mind one bit." He laughed.

But when she crossed her arms, he shook his head. "Okay, they might mind a bit, but this here is an important skill. Did you know that rodeo began as a way to celebrate all the daily tasks that keep a ranch going? Tying up calves could one day save that little one's life."

She had never thought of rodeos in quite that way. "And so your event celebrates these little guys."

"Exactly." He reached a hand out, and the calves ran away. "And that's just what we want in a calf. They need to run."

"I never would have thought of it like that." She reached a hand down, and one of them stepped tentatively closer.

"Nope. None of that. Come on, I'll show you who you can give some carrots to."

"I'm just making friends with the stars."

He shook his head. "Come on, you."

Kate hoped nothing about this day would move too quickly. She loved every minute of the barn, the animals, and her handsome tour guide. She'd missed him. How could one visit to New York from a stranger change her outlook on the very city she lived in? She saw him everywhere. Even flying out as she looked down at the park and the Statue of Liberty. He had left his mark. In more ways, and more places, than one.

After she had oohed and aahed over the pigs, they stepped back out into the sunlight. "I think it's time you met Pepper."

His large dog came running up and put both paws on his chest. "Hey, Sam." Dylan laughed and rubbed his dog's ears. His face lit and his eyes turned warm, and Kate's insides melted just a little bit.

"Sammy!" She reached out to touch his head.

He turned and licked her hand and then would have put his paws up on her, but Dylan said, "Down."

He immediately sat.

"Wow, he's obedient."

"He's a rodeo dog. He has to be, or they wouldn't let him around."

"Is he part of the show?"

"Sometimes. The county or fair shows. He can do some of the acts with the clowns. But for these professional contests, his job is to help out behind the scenes or stay out of the way."

She got down lower and rubbed his ears and his head. "He's beautiful."

Dylan grunted. "He might prefer something a little more manly. Sammy and I go way back."

She stood. Sam trotted along at Dylan's side as they entered the next barn. "Let's walk through here. Pepper's on the other end."

A horse whinnied and Kate sucked in a breath. A long row of stalls stretched in front of her. Every now and then the soft nose of a horse leaned over the edge.

"Look at all these beauties."

"We're at half capacity today. Spots are reserved for rodeo participants."

As soon as they approached the first stall, a horse popped his head over the stall door.

"Wow, you're friendly."

"It's almost showtime. They can feel it."

"Really? Do they like being in the rodeo?"

"I think so. Some do. Pepper loves it. I think he thinks it's all about him."

She laughed. "So your event is really about who's cooler, you or your horse?"

He shook his head. "Come on." He walked in the direction of Pepper's stall but did not get very far. The next horse popped her nose out too.

Kate had to pet them all, know their names, talk to them. She was in love with every horse in the barn. "They're magnificent. It's been too long since I have ridden."

He stood at her side. Their hands touched as he rested his palm on the side of the horse she was rubbing. "You're something, Kate."

"A good something?"

"Definitely. Something very good."

She turned to him, and he tucked a hair behind her ear. "Thanks for coming out."

She nodded, trying not to lean into his hand. "Wow."

His eyes turned knowing. But his lips quirked in a sort of

crooked smile. "Wow?" The questioning tilt of his head, half taunting, half challenging, made her stand taller.

"You're just a bit much for me, cowboy."

He tipped his head back and laughed. "I like that. There's something just right about what you said there." His grin grew. "I've decided not to be surprised by anything you say."

"Probably a good move."

"No, really, you're just so refreshing after...well, after every other person. I've never met anyone quite like you."

Her face was burning. Her hands tingled. She didn't know what to do with her feet 'cause she was sure she'd trip again, so she just sort of rocked in place.

But then he jerked his head. "Come on. If we don't start moving through this barn, we won't even get to meet my horse before I have to go get ready."

"Oh, right."

He picked up the pace, and even though her hands itched to pet every horse they passed, she kept up with him until he stopped in front of a larger stall.

Pepper came immediately to Dylan and rested his nose on the man's chest. As he embraced his horse, Kate didn't think she'd seen anything more moving. She snapped a picture with her phone.

After a moment, Pepper turned to her, his ears forward as he nickered.

"Ah, he likes you."

She sucked in a breath in wonder. "How do you know?"

"Well, those ears mean he's curious. I just know, besides."

She reached her hand out; winning over this horse was suddenly the most important thing in the world.

Pepper walked toward her and pressed his nose into her palm.

"Well I'll be."

Kate hardly moved. "What?"

"He really does. He likes you."

Out of the corner of her eye, she could see Dylan shaking his head in amazement, and it filled her with a sense of accomplishment. But she kept her main focus on Pepper. "There's a good boy. You gonna ride? You gonna help your sorry master rope something?"

Pepper's head bobbed for a moment and then he nudged her. "You looking for something?"

"Oh right." Dylan handed her a carrot. "And now your relationship will be solidified."

She fed Pepper a carrot and then rubbed his neck. She scratched the white diamond on his head and marveled at how velvety soft his nose was. "Who's my new love? Hmm? Who's my new love?" She handed her phone to Dylan. "Could you take a picture of me and Pepper?"

He stepped back, his expression unreadable, but he took the pictures while she posed with his horse. When he handed back her phone, she still hadn't figured out what he thought of all this. "What?"

"Hmm?"

"You're looking at me funny."

"I am? I'm sorry." He took off his hat and messed with his hair. "I just can't decide how to feel about you and my horse."

She kissed that velvety nose and then turned to Dylan. "What do you mean?"

He took her hand in his and placed it on the crook of his arm like people did in the olden times. She liked it.

"I think I might be jealous."

Her laugh caused a few more horses to poke their noses over the edge of their stalls.

Pepper nickered again behind them. And then nudged her again with his nose.

Dylan nodded. "I do believe I'm jealous."

"Jealous?" Her heart picked up its pace.

"Yep. I can't believe it, but I am."

"What on earth are you jealous of? Surely you don't think Pepper likes me better."

He shook his head. "Nope. Well, he better not. Ungrateful animal." They kept walking. They were almost to the end of the barn. "I'm jealous of all that attention you're giving to Pepper." He stepped in front of her. "And suddenly seeing you with my horse, him taking to you the way I did when I first met you, I realized some important things."

She held her breath. He was close enough to embrace, to kiss. She swallowed.

"Don't you want to know what I realized?"

Her nod was all she could manage for a reply.

"I realized I like it when you're here." He took her hand and toyed with her fingers for a moment as if he might say more, but then he laced their fingers together and he kept walking out of the barn.

Totally unsure what to think, she clutched his hand in the most nonchalant manner she could muster. Tingles of awareness flooded her arm, and she couldn't do anything but smile. Man, she hoped she didn't look like an idiot, walking along smiling.

"Want to go riding?" His voice was soft, deep.

She nodded.

"Okay, first thing tomorrow. Tonight we have the fire. How long are you staying?"

Forever? All month, at least. "My flight leaves tomorrow night."

"That's right. Okay. We'll have to squeeze in as much rodeo as we can."

His words said rodeo, but his hand cradling hers said, time with you. And she clung to that thought as the whole newness of this direction for them settled in around her.

Then she laughed, finding her voice at last. "And don't forget I get my own roping show."

"That you will." He tipped his hat. "I never forget a promise to a lady."

Kate knew those words would stick with her a long time.

CHAPTER 13

*D*ylan sat up on Pepper, trying to concentrate. Kate was in the audience. He knew right where she would be sitting. Kate. He tried to clear his mind, but it was no use. She'd firmly taken a spot in there once Pepper had loved her.

Dylan had never seen anything like it with his confounded horse. It's like Dylan had stopped existing and Kate was the center of his horse's newly besotted world. "You old sap," he muttered to himself or the horse or the universe, he wasn't sure. But this new swirl of emotions was confusing to say the least. Kate. Shelby? Kate was so much more than Shelby ever was. Not to mention Kate called him back and came to visit. And Kate. He would have kissed her if it hadn't been the most ridiculous idea his head had thought of in months. They'd not really been on one official date. He couldn't go kissing the woman with nothing to go off of as far as a relationship. His time spent in the Bible came back in a rush of understanding. Was his path opening up? He shook his head. Time would tell.

But from the way his heart hammered and his mind fixated solely on her, he'd better start actually getting to know the woman because he wasn't sure how long he wanted to wait before he pulled her into his arms and kissed her thoroughly.

Emboldened by his own thoughts, he laughed to himself. "It all starts at the campfire."

Pepper shifted below him, and Ted, the man working the gate, eyed him. "Everything okay over there, boss?" He called everyone boss.

Dylan patted Pepper. "Better than okay." He turned his thoughts to where they needed to be. Exhilarated by the freedom to pursue another woman, thrilled that she sat in the stands watching him, his focus tripped into immense intensity and he shifted his weight forward. Pepper's muscles rippled as he adjusted his weight. They were ready.

The calf took off, running into the arena. In a burst of animal power, Pepper was right behind. Dylan spun the rope above his head. As soon as they were close enough, he threw it and caught the calf right where he'd planned.

He leapt from his horse. His hands working faster than they ever had, he wrapped the calf's ankles, pulled the knot tight, and stood.

Six seconds, thirty. Wow, he'd never roped a cow that quickly.

His hands went up into the air as the crowds cheered. His time was blinking up on the boards. His eyes found Kate. He almost held his hand out, pointing in her direction, but he stopped. Instead he touched his hat and grinned. She waved.

As he made his way back out of the arena, the calf ran by and kicked up his heels as he did. Some in the audience caught it, he assumed, because they laughed. But he just shook his head. With one last wave, he and Pepper stepped out of the arena.

His coach stood just out of the way, his face beaming.

"Trev." Dylan nodded his head.

"You did it. You broke your record."

"That's something, isn't it?"

"Yeah it is, especially since the record you broke before that hadn't been broken in ten years."

"We're getting you to the Olympics. After you do a winning sweep across the nation."

"Sounds about right." He enjoyed talking to his coach, loved to hear his plans, but Dylan's mind buzzed with a new awareness of Kate sitting up there in the stands. It had been years since he'd sat in the stands in between events. And he didn't think he'd start doing it today, but man, he wanted to. And that said a lot.

"I think we need to start doubling in on the practices. Maybe we can work on what you did today, get it stuck so you can get it on repeat."

"Those are great ideas, Coach, but today I got some company visiting. I have a ride planned for the morning, but tomorrow night I'm all yours."

The coach opened his mouth to say something, Dylan could only guess what, but then he closed it again. "Tomorrow it is." He turned. "And have fun tonight."

"I think I will." Dylan led Pepper back to his stall in the arena, ready to rub him down and reward him. They'd been in perfect sync. He couldn't have done any of it without his horse. "Good boy. That was some show we gave them, wasn't it?"

He and Pepper did amazingly in all their other events. Standing up on the award podium never felt so good. Kate was right across from him clapping and jumping like she'd won it all herself. As much as he loved his accomplishments that day, everything about the evening was focused so intently on Kate he wondered if he even cared about the rest of it. Is this what it felt like to be falling for a woman? It had been so long, he couldn't remember.

After he'd taken care of Pepper, showered up, and collected wood for their fire, he finally saw Kate.

She stepped out of her trailer wearing some jean shorts that hugged her just right and a white T-shirt. Something about the way she stood there, watching him, made him want to run over and scoop her up into his arms.

His eyes travelled down her legs, and then he stopped. "You're wearing boots."

She nodded. "Sure am, cowboy. Am I doing it right?" She posed for a moment, drawing attention to her legs and boots and...hips. He swallowed.

"Now, you just come over to our fire. It's torture for you to go standing around looking all pretty and far away."

"You say the awesomest things."

He paused in placing the wood. "Do I?"

"Yeah, people don't talk that way anymore."

"Well, maybe they should."

She made her way over to stand in front of him. He rose. And she suddenly looked a little insecure. "Or you could just keep talking."

"I can do that." The pause was comfortable. He enjoyed their closeness, but they had to get this fire going. "But first, let's get some hot cocoa brewing and make some s'mores."

"You brought hot dogs too?" She lifted up the sack of food he'd placed on a log nearby.

"Oh, I did. But those are good hot dogs, not the funny pink ones. You're welcome to a good sausage dog as well if you like them."

"Only when cooked by a fire...or at a baseball game."

"And now we are truly the same person."

The warmth of her expression did more than the fire to add a sense of home and family. Then she shrugged. "What can I do?"

"You can just sit right there and keep looking just like you do. Oh, and tell me what you thought about your first rodeo."

She crossed her legs, and he had to refocus on the wood. Goodness, she was something. He kept saying that. But he'd never met someone he connected with so easily and who ignited in him a desire to be good while at the same time looking the way she did. Even though she was shorter than some women, her legs went on and on and on. He laughed at himself.

"I think I could spend my life just watching rodeos."

"So you liked it?"

"Oh, yeah. It was amazing. I thought that the bulls were going to be my favorite event."

He snorted. Everyone loved the bull riders.

"But then this one hot cowboy came riding out on the most beautiful horse I've ever seen." She shook her head. "Once a woman sees Pepper, her heart is lost forever."

His snort repeated itself, louder.

"But the rider, he was not so bad either."

"You did say something about him being hot."

She stopped and seemed to forget how to close her mouth. "Did I?"

"Yep, you certainly did."

"Oh, well, that just sort of slipped out."

"Then it's even more true."

She started to nod but then paused. "It could be."

"Could be?"

"Well, sure. A truly hot cowboy would have to be appealing in more ways than one."

"Oh, this is getting good. I can't wait to hear the rest of this conversation. Tell me first, do you want one or two dogs?"

"Just one."

He handed her a stick with a large sausage poked onto the end.

"Thank you."

She scooted her chair closer to the fire.

He sat beside her, and even though there were no coals or

glowing embers to use to cook, they held their sausages out over the flame.

"So, you were saying…" His eyebrows lifted in such an open and endearing way, she knew she was a goner.

"Hmm? Was I saying something?"

He growled. "Woman, you were talking about how a man has to be, and I'm more interested in those words than just about anything, so I hope you're ready to share." His gaze really found a home deep inside her, one she hoped he would take up residence in and stay for a while.

"Well, okay. I was thinking that a man is even more hot when he's the real deal."

He waited.

"Like, he's comfortable talking about God."

He nodded slowly.

"And he's good to others, kind."

He nodded again.

"And he's honorable."

"So, if I show you my old and well-read Bible, you're gonna be impressed."

She wrinkled her nose. "Not as much as if I see you just living a good and solid life, if I can tell you love Jesus just by the way you are."

"But what if I really did love Jesus a few years ago, but now I sort of don't think about him as much as I should?" He wanted to be honest with her, and he just didn't think that a man's faith should be used as a tool to win over women.

"I'd say you were honest. Which is another thing that makes a man hot."

"I'm beginning to think it might be hard to qualify."

"I mean, I think I already admitted you are." She sucked in a breath. "I keep saying things." She looked away, the fire's glow flickering off her face.

"I like it when you say things."

"But…"

"But?"

"I still haven't seen my own personal roping demonstration."

"True. After our ride in the morning, Pepper and I will happily rope whatever you tell us to. And then I win."

"What do you win again?"

"I'm not sure. We'll have to talk about this."

Her hotdog popped. It's juice dribbled down and sizzled in the fire.

"That smells so good. I just realized I'm starving."

He collected it with a bun and handed it to her. When their fingers grazed, she smiled, enjoying the buzzing up her arm.

"There's mustard and ketchup in the bag."

They settled in their chairs, Dylan cooking more hot dogs while he ate the one in his hand.

"Tell me about Decker."

He nearly choked. He forced a large chunk of hot dog down and drank deeply from his bottled water. "My brother?"

"Sure. You have a twin, right?"

"I do. Sure, I'm happy to talk about him."

The expression she sent him was more than confused, and he knew he was being weird about his brother. But he couldn't help but remember the nudge he had felt about introducing her to Deck, about how well she would fit in his family. Shelby came to mind. If he was going to work anything out with that woman, Kate really would be better off with Deck. But no. He pushed aside the odd train of thought and tried to be more chill about the whole thing. "Sorry. I'm not sure why that hot dog went down the way it did. Decker is awesome."

"I bet all your brothers are."

"It's true. But Deck. He's special. He's like me…but he's not. He works harder than most of us, he's one hundred percent motivated by duty, loves hard, works hard. He's…well, he's dang near perfect." He studied her out of the side of his eye.

"So, pretty much exactly like you?"

The gratitude that surged through him focused itself on her. But he had to correct her. "Nah. He's a one of a kind. Like any twin, I suppose we are related. But he's awesome. Most days I wonder how I can be more like my brother."

"That's awesome."

"And he's not married either." He forced the words out, but her reaction was a bit unsettling.

Her smile grew and she studied his face. "Now, why did you feel the need to tell me that?"

So she was going to ask the hard questions. "I don't know. It wasn't easy. I sort of wanted to make up a long-term relationship for him." Was it fair to call dibs on a woman? Probably not.

"Well, I want to meet him."

"You do?"

"Of course. The idea of another guy so much like you? I hardly believe it."

"You could come visit." The words were hardly out when he realized how bold they sounded, but she didn't seem at all affected by them.

"Okay."

They talked and laughed and sat in the quiet. They were cozy. And he liked that. But the later the hour, the more he watched her face, the more he knew he wanted more than cozy.

When she stood up to call it a night, he joined her. "Before you slip away, let me show you my ropes."

"Oh right."

"I can just do a few challenges tonight. And if they don't convince you, then next time you pick anything at all."

"This I gotta see."

"Sure you're not too tired?"

"For a roping challenge by you? Never." She followed him over to his trailer.

He dug out the ropes, cradling them in his hands. "These

right here, there as familiar to me as almost anything." He tied a loose lasso knot and then started to spin it in the air. "See, first thing you learn is just simply this. The idea is to let it float up there."

"That's cool."

He nodded. "So, see anything you want me to tie?"

She looked around. "How about that fence post top?"

"One fence post, coming up." He lifted the rope into the air and looped it over the post.

"That was way too easy." She crossed her arms. "How about that chair?"

"I'll do the arm rest on that camping chair."

"Oooh, Okay." Her eager stance, her very interest in his most favorite activity made him want to tie things all night.

He slipped the rope over the arm rest. Really, maybe he could show her some of the more challenging targets.

"Okay okay. I get it." Then she laughed. "Ha! How about a pop bottle." She picked up one from the cup holder and placed it on the ground.

"Now we're talking." He concentrated for a moment and then sent the rope over the bottle. When he pulled tight, the rope grabbed it. He exhaled. "I wasn't sure I could do that one. Well done."

She stepped closer. "No, *you* well done. This whole roping thing is pretty impressive."

"You saying you're impressed with me?"

"That's what I'm saying."

He reached for her hand. "I think I'd like to keep things that way."

"What way? Me impressed?"

"Yep. But hey, we can work on that some more tomorrow. Let me walk you to your door."

Instead of complaining that it was just ten feet away, she nodded.

Nobody was around. Looked like everyone had gone to bed, or cleared out at least, but he paused in the shadows of her temporary home. "Kate."

She looked up into his face, her eyes full. Her lips were so full and soft. He knew what he wanted. When his eyes found hers, he knew she wanted it too.

"Kate."

She nodded and stepped nearer. "Hmm?"

His arms encircled her, and before he even planned to, he was kissing her and she was responding as though she'd been wanting the same from him. Her soft mouth molded to his. Her hands rose up along his chest and circled his neck, sending rushes of energy through him. He pulled her closer, his palms cupping her hips. Her grip on his tightened and he knew.

He knew something special was about to happen.

CHAPTER 14

*D*ylan's phone buzzed in his pocket.

It was pressed against Kate, and she groaned at the interruption. She was brought too abruptly out of what felt almost like a dream. His arms encircled her as though she were precious. His mouth…his mouth caressed her, consumed her. She'd never felt this way about a man.

But his kisses slowed, and Kate reluctantly lowered her hands from his neck to his arms, accepting his kisses that were now soft and slow, as though he regretted the interruption. Then he paused. "Kate."

She whispered. "Wow."

"That's exactly what I was thinking." He stepped away, took her hand. "And the other thing I was thinking is that I should say goodnight."

"I don't think I can even leave after that."

"A man couldn't hear happier words than those." He opened her door. "Now, please, get yourself inside before I start thinking about anything else."

"Good night."

As soon as he shut the door, she wanted it opened. But

instead, she leaned against it, trying to slow her racing thoughts, calm her rush of energy, and stop herself from squealing out loud. What. A. Kiss.

Then she heard his voice. "Hey, Shelby."

"What?" She whipped around, alarm and hurt hammering through her, and peeked out her window. He was on his phone. She leaned her forehead against the glass, trying not to think. At least her roommate wasn't out there, which is what her brain had immediately thought. But was this any better? After a kiss like that, he was on the phone with his ex-girlfriend.

"Shelby, I don't have time for this right now. I'm sorry Kate's not there. Maybe call your mother?"

Kate smirked. Had Shelby called Dylan for one of the any number of things the woman always needed help with? Kate checked her phone. Yep. She'd called Kate too.

Dylan pocketed his phone. He looked for a long time at her trailer. She didn't think he could see her looking out the window. Then he doused their fire, making sure it was spread out and cold. He gathered all their things, picked up the place, and then headed to his own trailer. One whistle for Sammy, and the dog came running. She smiled at the wagging tail and then heard the door shut. "Goodnight," she repeated.

She woke up the next morning to about twenty texts from Shelby. The most worrisome stayed with Kate all the way to the airport, Dylan at her side. *I think I still love Dylan.*

She tried to push it aside, tried not to think about it, tried not to be ruled by it, but there it was. When she got out of the car, Dylan brought her bag to the curb and then tugged at her hand so that she was in his arms. "Come back."

She nodded. "Let's figure out a visit."

His lips found hers with a soft intensity that sent her clinging to him. And then she stepped away with her bag and walked through the airport doors.

I think I still love him.

Did Shelby remember that she was right there with Dylan? Kate stuffed her phone deep in the depths of her backpack and pulled out a book. But her thoughts plagued her.

Shelby could not possibly still love Dylan. She'd proved as much by the months and months she'd been dating someone else, and by the lack of attention she gave him when Dylan came to visit. She never talked about the guy. Kate had hardly known who she was talking about when she mentioned the visit to New York. Something must have happened. Maybe Ramon broke up with her. She groaned to herself. People nearby glanced in her direction, but she didn't care. If that had happened, Kate was going home to a needy, clingy Shelby who just might unleash all of that manipulation onto Dylan.

She made it back to New York and got a call in the cab while heading back to her apartment. "Kate, we need someone to take two conferences coming up. You're our first choice."

She knew why. Most of the agents didn't want to go to conferences. But she enjoyed it, and the whole needy, unhappy Shelby situation made for a perfect reason to skip town. "I'm in. Where?"

"San Antonio in a couple weeks. And Ohio in a couple months."

"Great. Set it up. Give me an extra week in San Antonio."

"A week? The conference is only three days."

She smiled. "I have friends in town."

"Got it, and thanks for doing these."

They hung up and she smiled. *San Antonio, here I come.*

As soon as she stepped into her apartment, she knew that Ramon had been there. The whole place reeked of his cologne. He stepped out of Shelby's bedroom. "Kate's back!" He looked over his shoulder.

Shelby waved. "How was it?"

"I'm in love with every horse in the place."

"Hey, well, I'm gonna run." Ramon stepped toward the door.

"Call me tonight?" Shelby's pout seemed terribly juvenile to Kate, but it seemed to work on men, some of them anyway.

"You know I can't. It's gonna be late when I get home." Ooh, perhaps Ramon was losing his fascination.

"I'll wait up." Her pout grew, and Kate looked away. She went to her room. As she unpacked, she tried not to hear Shelby's whiny demand for a phone call. Was this how she and Dylan worked things out? Did he jump to do everything she asked, or did he set some boundaries?

After another minute, the front area grew quiet. Then the door opened and closed. Kate piled up her laundry and slid her suitcase into its regular spot in the back of her closet. She thought she'd put in a load of laundry while she got caught up at work, but Shelby walked in and flopped down on Kate's bed. Her eyes were red. And she did look legitimately unhappy.

"Hey, now. Shelby, what's wrong?" She sat beside her.

"He doesn't love me anymore."

"Are you sure? He looked pretty attentive just now…"

"No, I have to beg to get him to call. He's probably dating someone else. That's the only reason he wouldn't want to do our goodnight call. We talk every single night before we go to sleep. And now, he doesn't want to?" Shelby closed her eyes, lying on her back.

"Is he acting normal otherwise?"

She sniffed. "He was. But tonight, he just looked like he was fed up."

"Maybe just do a test."

"What kind of test?"

What Kate was about to suggest just might save Shelby's relationship. "Don't tell him to call. Don't needle him or ask. Just go out with the guy. Text him 'thank you' after. And give him space."

"That's it? That's the test?"

"Then after a few days, see if he calls on his own." Kate

shrugged. "I bet he does. The man has been nothing but madly in love with you from the very first date."

Shelby smiled. "He has, hasn't he?" She sat up. "But then what if I do this test and he doesn't call? What if he forgets about me and I've lost my chance with him?"

"He's not going to forget about you. But, really, if he only calls because you tell him to, do you want that in your life?"

"Yes."

"No, come on. You deserve someone who wants to be with you just because you're you. Not because they feel obligated." Kate bit her lip. The words slipped out without thought. But Shelby didn't seem to notice that Kate suggested men only stayed with her out of obligation. That's not what she meant.

"You're right. If he doesn't want to call me, then why do I need him in my life? I've got Dylan." She hugged herself and her smile grew just as something sunk uncomfortably in Kate's stomach. Shelby turned to her. "Isn't he literally the best?"

Kate laughed, hoping it sounded real and not like a strangled kitten. "Yes, he's pretty great."

"Oh, you were too busy loving the horses." Shelby waved her hand. "But that man is everything a woman could want. I can't believe I ever let him go."

Kate now wanted to leave, to walk, to move, to be anywhere but here listening to Shelby talk about Dylan. The man who had just kissed her. The man who would be calling her that night before bed. Would he run back to Shelby if the woman started turning all this smiling, primping, whining attention back on him?

"Hey, so I'm gonna get this load in, and then I'm behind at work."

"Oh right. Always working. Ramon said the new guy at work is single. Let's double."

"Sure." Kate scooped up her clothes into a hamper and placed it on her hip. "You going out again tonight?"

Shelby sighed. "A group wants to meet at the Blue Saloon, but I don't know if I'm feeling it." She pulled out her phone. "Maybe I'll just call Dylan." She scrolled through pictures with a dreamy look on her face.

Kate left her on the bed.

She worked hard and probably had one of the most productive evenings of her career. With headphones in, she went through submission after submission with a vengeance, but she still found three good ones. And that was success. One she was particularly pleased with. It was a gem, and if Kate found the right publishing house, the book could make millions for somebody, probably not her, but it might jump-start her career.

Shelby walked back and forth in front of her workspace. Kate didn't know what she was doing. She just turned up her music.

And then, when Kate knew she'd have to stop again, her phone dinged. *Dylan!*

He texted, "Shelby says you're working hard."

Ugh. She stood up, grabbed her purse and walked out the door without another word. She pressed the call button.

"Kate!" His voice made everything feel a little better.

"Hey, I have news."

"Oh? I hope it's the kind that means you're coming back."

"Well, it's the kind that means I'm coming to San Antonio." She held her breath, listening for any change in tone.

"That's right where my family lives! I'll be training there. When?" The excitement, the sincerity in his voice further comforted her.

"Next week. Do you think Pepper misses me?"

"Pepper, Sam, and this other guy."

"Oh yeah? Did he miss me too?"

"Like his hat. He missed you like he does his hat." His voice was low and rumbly, and it rolled through her in a wave of desire.

"That's a lot of missing."

"Hmm. Come stay at the house. I can't wait for you to meet everyone."

"Oh, you sure? They have a hotel for me."

"No way. That's too far." He paused. "We have horses." The grin in his voice made her laugh.

"Well, I don't know if I can cheat on Pepper."

"Now that's a good point."

She hummed. "I'd love to stay with your family."

"And they're gonna love you."

"You think so?"

"Oh, for sure. The first thing I thought when I met you was how much you reminded me of the fam. In a good way. You're a lot like my mother."

"Is that really a good thing? A man only needs one mother in his life." She kept her voice light, but it was a valid concern, honestly.

"It's the best kind of thing. You're only like my mother in some ways. And not like my mother in some other very important ways."

"Miss you."

"Miss your mouth."

"Dylan." She laughed, looking around at people on the street. "Hush."

"No one can hear me."

"Okay, fine. I miss yours too."

His laugh was so triumphant, so utterly thrilled she couldn't help but join in. "Okay, stop. Now I'm embarrassed."

"No, no. Don't be embarrassed. I haven't had this much fun talking to a woman since..."

The pause lingered, and she hated every long, drawn out millisecond of it, but then his quiet voice sank deep inside.

"Well, ever. I've never had this much fun talking to a woman."

"You sure about that?"

"You sound like you don't believe me."

"I believe you. I guess."

"Yup. Definitely sounds like I'm gonna need to do some proving."

"I like the sound of that."

"I'm counting on you loving it."

"See you soon?"

"Send me your flight plans."

When they hung up, she just kept walking in a daze, reliving every single word. Could this really be happening? Could things be this wonderful between them? She hugged her phone to her stomach as she wrapped her arms around her waist and walked and walked until she noticed her surroundings and the dark silent streets and immediately called an Uber. But even though she got in super late, even though she didn't touch any more of her work, she couldn't regret one moment.

CHAPTER 15

*D*ylan moved his trailer, Pepper, and Sam to the new fairgrounds where he would be training for the upcoming season. He was close enough to home he could be there for Sundays, but far enough away he could really focus on his work without feeling like he needed to be the one mending the fences and cleaning up after the cows. The Dawson Ranch was a family-run establishment, and it really needed the full family support, but they had all discovered a few years back that the ranch did better with someone out riding rodeo. It spread the brand and drummed up sponsors as well as buyers of their beef and hay. And right now, it was Dylan's turn. If he could win, if he could be the first Dawson to snag an Olympic spot, the Dawson brand would be solidified in the professional rodeo and ranch world, and of course, he would be honored to represent the United States.

A rooster crowed outside his window. "That bird is gonna be dinner if he's not careful."

A shotgun rang out, rattling his ears. Sam whined. Dylan rested a hand on his loyal dog. "Dude!" Dylan shouted out to the old man. Dang that Scooter. He couldn't be shooting his gun whenever he wanted. San Antonio was not like his sprawling acreage out in West Texas.

"Missed." The man swore a few times, and Dylan could only agree with him, though perhaps without the expletives.

"Scooter, put that gun away or I'm taking it." His boss's voice sounded gravelly, like he'd been rattled awake by the gunfire.

Dylan smiled. This was gonna be one interesting go of things. The bull riders were on the opposite side of camp. They stuck together and had fancier trailers and, in some cases, better sponsors. He was sure they'd hear all about the rooster and the attempt on his life from them later today.

But neither roosters nor guns outside his window would wreck this day. He was going to the airport to pick up Kate in a few hours and then home to the ranch, where he could sit back and watch just how much Kate fit in there.

His phone rang. Without looking at the caller, he smiled into the device. "Hey, Kate."

Silence.

"Hello?"

"Dylan?" Shelby's voice, sounding more pouty than ever, whispered back.

"Hey, Bee. How's it going?"

"Oh, I'm fine, just a little lonely."

"I'm sorry."

"Kate's gone. She's got another writing conference. I swear, she's gone all the time now, and you know how I don't like to be alone."

He didn't know that. There was a lot he didn't know about her. "Well, hey, I can talk to you while you get ready for work, how's that?"

"I was kind of hoping you could come up here this weekend."

His mind went in a million directions. Isn't this what he'd been waiting for? An opportunity to truly win her back. But... he really wasn't sure that's what he wanted anymore. And Kate was coming. "Oh, shoot. I can't really do that. But what's keeping you there?" He knew he would regret this, but the words seemed to be rolling forth of their own volition. "I mean, if you're alone, come home. I bet your mama hasn't seen you in a long time."

"Do you think I should?"

"Why not? It's always good for a person to get a solid dose of Willow Creek, I say."

"And you'll be there."

"Well, mostly I'm at the San Antonio Fairgrounds. So I probably won't really see you much while you're here, but you sure won't be alone."

"But I was hoping I could see you."

"I'm sure we'll see each other. Anyway, I gotta run. Thanks for calling."

"Maybe I'll see you soon, then."

"Right. Bye."

Why had he told her to come home? It seemed like the best way to make her happy, surround her with the people who love her. But would she really do it? How many times had he or any of them wished to see her in Willow Creek again? That seemed like a terrible idea now that he was off the phone.

Instead of trying to divert her, perhaps he should have just told her he couldn't come to New York because Kate was gonna be in Willow Creek. But Kate hadn't told her, had she? Sometimes he couldn't tell with Shelby. She might know all about Kate but wasn't letting on. He stepped outside his trailer.

One of the most frustrating things about Shelby was that he could never tell when he was being manipulated. But he'd figured out a way for them to get on well together. He knew he could make things work with her, and for the longest time that had seemed like enough. Until he met Kate.

He brushed down Pepper, gave him food and water, and then called his mom.

"Hey, Dylan. I'm excited to have you home, son."

"Thanks. It's great I can train so close by."

"Tell me again about this Kate. I've got her in the corner bedroom so she has the best view up there. If that land doesn't make her fall in love with you, then maybe she's not meant to be a Dawson."

He laughed. "I'm not trying to make her fall in love with me."

"Then what are you doing?"

A quick joke on the tip of his tongue, he paused. "Well, I think I'm just trying to get to know the woman."

"Bringing a woman home to the family seems like a bit more than getting to know her."

"I know. It just worked out this way. We're friends." The feel of her in his arms niggled his conscious. "And a bit more." He laughed again. "Mom, we just don't know what we are. It's very new."

"Well, we're just gonna be Dawsons. And time will tell. But I have a good feeling about this one."

He smiled. "Mm. Me too."

A few hours later, he hopped in his truck, ready to head to the airport, and called Kate.

But of course she didn't pick up. Her flight wasn't in yet. He just wanted there to be a message waiting for her. "Hey, Kate. I'll be outside when you land. Can't wait to see you." There was so much more he would tell her if he could figure out the right words to let her know how much he enjoyed her company. Maybe he could find a way this weekend while she was in town.

He leaned up against the side of his truck, watching for Kate. The more he thought about it, the more he wished that this airport scene wasn't a normal thing for them. But they lived far apart. And New York really wasn't a place for a rodeo man. As far as he could tell, she loved her job and had no plans of quitting. Did New York agents ever live outside of New York? Like he'd told his mom, they didn't know much about where this would go, but he was hoping to find out.

His eyes searched the face of each new person. The crowd started to slow. He checked his phone. No messages. Then a high-pitched sort of grating sound carried over to him. "He's going to be so surprised. I love it when I surprise my boyfriend. Well, we aren't really dating anymore, but old habits die hard, I guess." Shelby? He looked up just as she approached with her arms out. "Here I am!" She stepped into his arms. All of her strawberry smelling, hair-sprayed self with bags and purses falling off her arms around her. "You are so good to come."

He shook his head, hardly responding to her hug. "What are you doing here?"

Out came her pout. "What are you talking about? You asked me to come." She shook her head. "Now, let's get this stuff in the truck. But not in the back, you know how I feel about all my stuff sliding around in the dirty bed."

Something clenched inside. His truck bed was immaculate. But whatever. "So, are you saying you need a ride home?"

She laughed as if he was being ridiculous.

But he didn't put her things inside. He stepped back up on the curb, ready to leave her with the truck while he went to find Kate.

She stood in the middle of the sidewalk, just outside the door, while people walked around and past her. Her bags were in hand, but she seemed frozen in place, probably taking in the scene behind him. He picked up his pace and reached her in moments. But before he could say a word, Shelby called from behind, "There you are, Kate. We've been waiting. I don't know how I beat you off the plane."

"Kate?" He leaned in to kiss her cheek. He wished he was swinging her up in his arms and holding her close.

She was stiff, her face completely blank. He picked up her bags and led her back to his truck. Shelby linked arms with her and started babbling. "I'm so happy to introduce you to my home. Aren't we happy she could come? Willow Creek is just so idyllic. Some people never leave. You'll see so many differences to New York, and I'm sure by the time you're done here, you'll be happy to get back, but it's just so fulfilling for those of us who were raised here." Shelby looked over at him as though to share some kind of bond.

But he was baffled—more than baffled. "Shelby."

She stopped talking. "Hmm?"

He just shook his head and tossed in her bags and then Kate's.

Shelby jumped into his truck, scooting to the middle and patted the seat for Kate to hop up beside her. Before she climbed in, Dylan reached for her hand.

When she turned, he winked, which earned him a small smile. Feeling more reassured, he closed the door behind her and shook his head. What was going on here? Well, one thing that wasn't going on—Shelby was not coming to his house.

When he started up the truck, he turned on the music. It was going to be a long ride from the airport to Shelby's.

She talked on and on and on about nothing. Had she always been like this? He couldn't remember. But right now, he just wanted to hear how Kate's week had been.

"So, Kate."

Shelby stopped. Kate looked in his direction.

"I was wondering, how was your flight?"

Amusement lit her face. "It was great. Much faster than I thought it would be."

He nodded. "New York doesn't seem so far when a quick flight will get you here."

"I suppose you're pointing that out 'cause I haven't been home much?" Shelby turned to Kate. "It's a bit of a sore spot. I can't blame him. But as you know, it's busy in New York. We don't have time to be flitting across the country every weekend, even for a boyfriend."

Dylan stiffened further and rotated his neck. Was now the time to set her straight? What was she trying to pull? "Actually I was pointing out to Kate how simple it would be to go back and forth between here and New York, 'cause I'd like to see her more."

Kate sucked in a breath.

But Shelby seemed not to even notice the pointed comment. "Of course, I think you could just as easily come to New York. And transportation there is so easy." She kept talking all about New York and the benefits of living there.

Dylan gave up participating in the conversation and just hoped Kate would hang in there until they could drop Shelby off.

One time he caught her eye, and her wide-eyed expression almost made him laugh.

After about forty-five minutes, he pulled in front of Shelby's house. He hopped out and moved around to the passenger door.

The front door opened. "Is that my Dylan?" Shelby's mother ran out, wiping hands on her apron.

"It is. Hello, Mrs. Hopkins."

"It's good to see you! Did I hear you'll be riding around here for a couple months?"

"Yes you did, ma'am. I'm training for a national tour."

"I always knew you'd be a star." She accepted a kiss on her cheek and then hugged her daughter. "Shelby, honey, welcome home."

"Thanks, Mother." She gave her a quick embrace and then walked on by toward the front door. "The bags can go in here."

Dylan turned to Kate. She waved him in.

"Now, who's in the car?" Mrs. Hopkins moved around to the side. So Kate opened the door.

"That's Kate Reece."

"My roommate. Mama, remember I told you about Kate?"

Judging by Mrs. Hopkins' face, Shelby might not have ever mentioned her, or not much.

"Oh well, I am so happy to meet you. Come on down here so I can welcome you properly." To Mrs. Hopkins, that meant a huge full hug. "Come on in. Are you staying here with Shelby?"

Kate shook her head. "Oh, no."

"Actually, Mrs. Hopkins. She's here for a writing conference."

"Well, you're always welcome here. Come back for Sunday dinner at least."

"Thank you, ma'am, but my mama would not forgive me if we didn't spend the meal at home." He carried the bags into the house and set them inside the front door.

Shelby tugged at him arms so that he let the front door close. Then she stepped close enough that he could kiss her if he liked. "Remember this doorway?" Her smile grew. "I have lots of fond memories right here."

He supposed she was talking about all the times he'd said goodbye at the door. For a moment, he smiled. "Course I remember." Then he stepped back. "I best be going."

"So soon? You and Kate can come in, stay awhile. Mama's made lemonade, I'm sure of it."

He shook his head. "My own mama's waiting on us."

Her hand tugged at his arm until he stepped out of her grip and back onto the porch. Mrs. Hopkins was still loving on Kate, and Dylan wasn't sure how any of this was going down with her.

"You come back now. We won't take no for an answer. Of course I want to feed Shelby's roommate. The two of you don't eat enough out there."

"Thank you, Mrs. Hopkins." Kate climbed back into the truck, and Dylan stepped up to close her door. "You are all kindness."

"Oh, it's good to see you. When you both left, everything got so much more lonely around here."

"I'm glad she's back. It's been a long time."

"Yes, it has." She stepped away. "Well, I won't keep you."

"I'm sure I'll be seeing you."

"Thanks for dropping her off."

He nodded and climbed in. Once the door was closed, he let out all the tense air that had been building up in his chest. "Sorry about that."

They kept their expressions placid while they waved to Mrs. Hopkins. Shelby was still inside.

But when they at last reached the top of the driveway and were out of sight, he turned to Kate with a half growl. "Now, you scoot right on over here." His hand pulled at her and moved her to sit beside him. "You can put a seatbelt on right there, little lady, and I'll start to feel a bit better about things."

She clicked in her buckle and then leaned into him just enough. "Wow, that was something."

"Did you know she was coming?" he asked.

"Not until she stepped out of her room this morning and asked if we could share a ride to the airport." She was quiet for a moment. "She said you invited her."

The question in the air needed an immediate answer. He looked in his rearview mirror. No one was coming on the long country highway. He pulled over to the side of the road. "She called me this morning, moaning about you not being there and about how she was going to be lonely. She wanted me to come to New York."

"So you told her to come here?"

"Well, I told her to come visit her parents and that I would likely not see her much but that lots of people in town would be happy to have her back."

Kate nodded slowly.

The question he wanted to know the answer to was one she

was probably asking herself—now what? "I'm just happy you're here. How much time do you have outside of that conference of yours?"

"I have every day really. I just need to be there to hear pitches, and I'm teaching one workshop on which kinds of books my agency is most looking to represent."

"So you have time to come by the fairgrounds?"

"Oh, yes."

"And time to ride horses?"

"A double yes." Her smile grew.

"And time to spend at the ranch with me and my family."

"Yes." Her eyebrows furrowed for a second and then cleared.

He started up the truck again but didn't move. "I imagined our meeting at the airport a little differently."

"Yeah, me too." She looked away.

"I'm sorry this is a bit awkward. I found a surprising gift when I went to New York."

She turned back to him.

"And I don't want to lose you, not yet."

She searched his face for a moment and then nodded. "I'm not going anywhere."

"I mean. We don't know what this is—other than great—and you live there, and I live all over, but…"

She held up a hand. "But it is worth it to find out."

He nodded, relieved. "Exactly." He looked behind, ready to pull out onto the road. "Things with you are so much easier."

"Than Shelby?"

He sighed. "I don't want to be comparing you all the time. It's just that every time, every talk, every*thing* with you just seems to fit. And with her it's always a struggle."

As he was about to pull out, her hand on his arm stopped him, and then she leaned across and kissed him.

"Mmm." He pulled her close, as close as he could, and responded as though he'd been living in a kiss desert, which was true. When she pulled back, she sighed, and a slow smile lit her face.

"Now that's better."

She nodded.

He headed down the road toward the Dawson ranch with a lighter heart.

Her hand reached for his, and their laced fingers resting there in her lap felt more right than anything else that morning.

Shelby's arrival was a complication, but seeing Kate's hand in his gave him a warm confidence that they could make it work.

CHAPTER 16

Their drive became prettier and prettier the closer they got to the Dawson ranch. The trees turned to pine. The road became less flat and more hilly. The autumn colors were starting to come out on the trees. And then he turned in to a long drive under a Dawson Ranch sign. The electronic gate shut again behind them. The drive was lined with two white fences that seemed to go for miles to the front and out in either direction everywhere she looked.

"And here they come." Dylan watched as a cloud of dust moved their way.

She followed his gaze and unbuckled immediately at the sight of a whole herd of horses running toward them.

"You wanna get out here?"

"Yes. Can we?" She was already scooting over to the door.

He chuckled and pulled over to the side of the driveway. Before he could get out to open her door or even walk over in her direction, she was out of the truck and up on the fence, reaching out to the nearest horses.

"Hey there, buddy." The first horse, black with such a shiny coat, nuzzled her. "I don't have anything for you." She reached her hand over above his nose.

More came over, pushing and bumping each other to greet Kate. Dylan stood beside her and then reached down and grabbed a handful of grass. "Here, feed them this."

She took it. "Aren't they amazing!" The wonder, love, and excitement she felt for a bunch of horses came from deep inside. She knew her eight-, nine-, ten-year-old self would be dead right now. And to honor all those years of craving horses, she lived it up now. She loved them even now. "They're so beautiful."

"You make me appreciate my home like I never have before."

"You've got something real special here. Not many get to have this, you know?"

"I thought you loved New York." He stood up beside her on the bottom fence rail.

"I do. It's my dream come true to be an agent out there. But…" She shrugged and reached for another soft nose. "I never get to do this." How could she explain how cool it was to someone who got to do it every day?

She could feel him watching her, and she smiled. "Thanks for letting me come."

"Hey, anytime. If you didn't love New York so much, I'd tell you to move in."

She laughed but didn't answer. He couldn't be serious. They hardly knew each other. But the idea sounded amazing. For a month. But not forever. She'd have to go into the office in New York enough that it would make travel complicated. She stopped. Why was she analyzing a plan to make it work? She reached for another horse. Because she was surrounded by gorgeous horses with a handsome cowboy at her side. She shook her head. "My younger self would die right now. Dead."

He laughed. "I get it. It's something you've always loved." His shoulder bumped hers. "Like the first time I roped something."

She nodded. "Or the first time I helped an author sign a deal with a publisher. Everyone's dreams coming true at one time."

People at the house were starting to come out on the porch. He waved. And she did too. "That your family?"

"Yep."

She laughed. "Do they think I'm a crazy city girl who's never seen a horse before?" She stepped down, waving to them again.

He squinted. "Now, let me see. That's Mama, and who's to know what she's thinking. The best of you, that's for sure, beyond that, she'll tell you. And looks like Nash is out there. He's the youngest. He gets a lot of lip from all of us because he deserves it."

"But a lot of love from your mama?"

"How did you know?"

She shrugged. "Lucky guess."

"Hm." He stepped back over to the truck. "Well, come on. Let's get you over there so you can meet them all."

Decker stepped out.

"Ah, and that must be Decker."

"And how did you know that from all the way over here?" Dylan squinted to take a look.

"Cause he stands just like you."

"Does he?" He shook his head. "Do I do that cool hands in the pockets thing he's doing right now?"

"Yes, you do, cowboy."

"Huh."

She stood up on the step at her door. "I got it."

He shook his head. "Oh no."

"What?"

"Mama would have my hide. We ride inside the car. Family rule."

"And you boys always do what your mama says?"

"You know it. At least, when she's standing there watching." He winked.

"Got it."

They drove the rest of the way up the long driveway, and by the time they got to the house, Maverick, Bailey, and Grace had joined the others. "And here's the whole gang."

She hopped out and was immediately smothered by Dylan's mama. "Now you just come on in. We have the corner bedroom all ready for you. Dylan says you're working, so you just shut that door and we will leave you be." She waved her hand. "Boys, get her luggage."

"I don't have much." She laughed, loving this woman. Something about her felt an awful lot like home.

Dylan picked up her suitcase and Decker took her duffle.

"This is Decker, Nash, Maverick."

Three tall men nearly smothered her next. Unless she tipped her head way back, she was looking straight at their chests. She didn't know what to do with so many huge men. "Good to meet you guys."

Then Bailey stepped forward. "I'm Maverick's wife, and this is our girl, Grace."

"Good to meet everyone. Wow. I'm so happy to be here."

"Turns out Kate has been wanting to come visit a ranch for a long time."

"Well you've come to the right place. The Dawson ranch has been a real working ranch for almost a hundred years."

"That's amazing."

"We haven't been doing the same kinds of ranching all that time, but we've been around."

"Now that's true, isn't it? We were dairy farming for a while, and we grew some different food crops for a while. But we've always had hay." Mama ushered them in. "But someone can give her a tour and tell her all that later. Come on in. Let's get some dinner on the table."

Kate looked from one to the other, just drinking in what it

would be like to be a Dawson, to live in a real ranch house, to own horses. She followed them into the house.

Dylan took her hand in his. "Overwhelmed?"

She shook her head. "Nope. This is great."

"I knew it."

"What?"

"That you'd love it here."

She smiled and they all moved into a dining room that had the largest wood table she'd ever seen.

"Now, this table's seen a lot of use. But we wouldn't trade it for anything. It fits us and our loved ones and friends, and that's just the way Mama likes it."

"It's perfect." She looked around at everything and everyone, and she meant it. They sat and everyone held hands.

"Dylan," Mama called over to her son.

Everyone bowed their heads. Dylan's hand squeezed hers twice.

"Dear God. We are so thankful to be here together. We're thankful for this family and for our father who is no longer here with us. Thank you for watching over each of us. Thank you for our mama who keeps us all in line. And for each Dawson. We're so happy Kate could come visit, and we ask that thou bless her in her efforts that she can be successful at work. We ask for suffering to cease and that we will do our part to help the world be a better place…"

He continued for a long time. She was expecting a quick little prayer about blessing the food, but he went on and on. His words touched her. She peeked at the others around the table. Each had their head bowed, and even the young girl, Gracie, was concentrating.

She caught Nash's eye, and he winked, which made her almost snort. But she kept quiet and returned to listening carefully. The more he prayed, the more she realized how grateful she was for a man who prayed to God. At the end, when he said amen, everyone repeated, "Amen."

Then they all looked at Mama.

"Your papa would be real proud of you boys and Bailey, Grace, and Kate too. We miss him, but we know he's smiling down on us and helping us when we need a swift kick."

Did Kate imagine it, or did she look extra-long at Nash?

He just smiled as large as ever while Mama looked at each in turn and then said, "Let's eat."

They passed the food around, and before long, she had a plate so full of food she knew she'd never eat it all. "This is like Thanksgiving."

"It sure is." Decker grinned and poured some extra gravy over his potatoes. "The beef is from one of our cows."

Kate had potatoes, asparagus, a thick steak, and a soft roll on her plate. Still on the table was a delicious-looking green salad, Jell-O, and what looked like a shrimp pasta salad. As she watched each of the boys get huge helpings of everything, she had to hand it to their mother. She knew how to feed men.

"Straight to a man's heart." Mrs. Dawson winked at Kate.

"I can see that." She laughed then turned to Bailey. "How long have you known the family?"

"Oh, I grew up here. Maverick and I dated in high school."

"That is the coolest story." She smiled and then remembered that Dylan had dated Shelby. "Do all of you marry your high school girlfriends?"

Nash shook his head. "Do you see any other wives sitting at this table?"

"No sir." Kate liked Nash. She suspected a lot more went on in his head than he let on.

"I think I'll take Kate riding after dinner."

"Oh, that's a great idea. The sun's been giving us some amazing sunsets this week."

"Thanks, Mama."

"Tell us what you do, Kate." Bailey poured herself some more water.

"I'm a literary agent. I help authors find publishers to sell their books."

"So if Decker and I write a book, you can help it get sold to a publisher?"

"If it's a really good book, sure."

"What's a book you have sold?"

"Well, I'm new. But I've sold children's books and some young adult. I might get a really amazing deal for this one author. I can't tell you yet, but when I do, you will have heard of her."

"That's wonderful." Mama smiled.

"What do you do, Bailey?"

"I am the choir teacher at the school."

"And she produces her own music."

"That's incredible. Have I heard any of your songs?"

"If you like country, you've heard of our Bailey." They started singing a popular song that had been on repeat on the radio for the past couple months. Kate joined in laughing. "Wait, no way. You sang that?"

"I did."

"She wrote it too." Maverick put his arm on the back of her chair.

"I'm super impressed. That's one of my favorites."

"Thank you. I'll send you home with the album if you like."

"Yes. I'd love that."

"I know no one uses CDs anymore, but maybe it will be in a museum one day or something."

They finished up dinner and everyone chipped in to clean the table. With what looked like no coordination at all, everyone had a job and the dishes were getting done.

She dried off the last plate, still in partial awe at the Dawson family. "That was incredible."

"Mama is the best cook, honestly."

"Yes, I loved the food, but I mean all of it. You guys work together, clean up, everything."

"Well, we've been doing this for a whole lotta years. Every Sunday, if we can make it, we're sitting right here and washing right there." Decker laid his own towel down on the counter. "Father never let Mama touch a dirty dish."

Kate followed Dylan back out toward the front door. "You might want a jacket." He took one off the coat rack. "Wear this."

It sort of drowned her, but it smelled like heaven. She breathed in the scent of it as Dylan watched her.

"It smells like you."

"Huh."

"Huh what?"

"Well, that's my jacket."

"Didn't I say it smells like you?"

"Yeah, come on." He grabbed her hand and laced their fingers together. "Let's get you saddled up before you spend another five minutes on a real ranch with horses."

"That's what I'm talking about. But after that, can we go running?"

"Need to run off some of that dinner?"

"I better."

"Yep. I'll run with you."

"Awesome."

They entered the barn and Kate took another deep breath. "This smells awesome too."

"Now that's my kind of girl."

She smiled, laughing to herself as she imagined Shelby in here. And then she stopped. Shelby had told her that she rode horses and even won some kind of competition growing up. Shelby probably looked great up on a horse. The problem with being here at Dylan's home was that everywhere she looked, Shelby had already been there.

"Okay, here's Tempest. She's a real sweetheart." He held out the reins.

She took them. "What do I do?"

"Just talk to her for a minute while I get this other horse saddled up."

"Got it." She placed a hand up on Tempest's nose. "We gonna be friends? I wanna go for a ride, but it's been a real long time. Help a girl out?"

Tempest whinnied. And Kate laughed.

"You guys having some kind of joke over there?"

"She's giving me all your secrets."

"I wouldn't be surprised that Tempest knows everything."

Dylan came walking out, leading a really tall horse.

"And this is Champ. He's a solid guy and he listens. Usually." Champ moved over to Tempest. "And he likes Tempest, so it helps that we take them out together."

"Do some of the horses not like each other?"

"Oh yeah, just like people. And they're always trying to decide who's the boss."

"And who wins?"

"Usually the mares." He laughed. "Unless there's a stallion around."

He brought her over to a block. "Step up on here to mount. Do you remember how?"

"I think so." She stuck her left foot in the stirrup, swung her other leg up, and before she knew it, she was sitting up on a horse again. "This is so cool." Her voice was hushed, like she didn't want to scare her horse.

"We're gonna ride out to the ridge to see the sunset. We'll be coming home in the dark, but these guys know where to go."

"Sounds great to me. Whatever we do, I'll think it's fantastic."

He rode over to her, and the horses started walking side by side out of the barn and out into the paddock. "The one rule around the house?"

"Besides you ride inside the car?"

He nodded. "You always close the gate." He swung down and walked his horse out the gate. Tempest followed, and then he swung the gate closed and secured it. "No one wants their horses running all over the front property."

"Got it. Shut the gate."

She didn't think life could get any more amazing than at that moment. If she thought Dylan was great in New York, he just became unbelievably so here on his property. Probably sometime soon, she was going to need to take a look at her roommate situation, her feelings for Dylan, and her job in New York, and decide if all this time with a cowboy was a real thing or a girlish fantasy playing out. Because New York was important to her, being fair to her roommate was important, and if those things mattered more, resisting Dylan would just get more and more difficult as time went on.

CHAPTER 17

*D*ylan couldn't stop looking at Kate up on a horse. "You sure you don't do this all the time?"

She leaned back and smiled. "I wish."

They moved along the back fields, following the horse trails at the edge of the hay crops. The fence was on their right and open fields on their left. He was taking her up to the top of the ridge, and to get there, they would go through the fields and the trees at the back and then up a rocky climb to the top. Her horse was sure-footed and had taken the same path a hundred times.

"So tell me, Kate. You look good on that horse. Do you ever see yourself stepping away from all that big city life and getting your own bit of land?"

She didn't say anything for a long time. "Are you asking just in fun, or are you seriously asking?"

"Well, it was more of a casual question, you know, like where do you see yourself in five years? But seeing you up on that horse tweaked the question in my favor." He grinned.

"In fun, totally. I can see myself leaving it all and getting a place with my own horse. I don't even need more than one. I could do my work remotely, and I'd love living somewhere with all this space and quiet." She looked out over his ranch, the land of his fathers for generations. And he wondered if she felt the same peace there that he did.

"And not in fun?"

Her sigh was heavy sounding. "I don't know if I could ever leave New York."

Though he didn't particularly like the sound of that, he could understand. "I don't think I could leave the rodeo yet either."

She nodded.

"It's my dream, you know? To succeed the way I am, to win. To get that Olympic spot. No Dawson brother has pursued things as far as I have."

"Maverick has all kinds of records though, right?"

"Yes. Mav's a legendary bull rider. Just about everywhere I go, people know Mav."

"Your dream keeps you on the road."

"And yours keeps you in New York."

They rode quietly for a moment before she spoke again. "But I've seen you more than almost anyone else." She grinned. "I'm not sure if I should encourage that or not, but it's been nice." The question in her eyes was unmistakable.

"I agree. So I guess we don't worry about the five-year plan right now."

"Just take it day by day?"

"I like that. All I know is I've missed you every day since the last time I saw you."

The light in her eyes at his comment made him happy.

"And I like the look of you on a horse, those two things."

"Well, we already know how in love I am with the horses and the ranch and...everything."

"And the cowboy on the horse?" He couldn't resist.

Her cheeks turned pink. "Yes, and the cowboy on the horse. I like him too." She laughed. "Now, come on. Do these horses know how to run?"

"Oh yeah they do!" He nudged Champ with the barest squeeze of his thighs. They leapt forward, racing across the ground, Kate keeping up with him gate by gate. Even though he did this for a living, even though he rode every day, there was something different about flying across his property with Kate.

She shouted to the wind, "I love this!" Her hair flew out behind her, her smile full and happy. In that moment, she was probably the most beautiful thing he'd ever seen.

He spurred his horse faster. "Yeeeehaw!"

They laughed and rode, and the horses seemed to pick up the mood and leapt in their steps as they raced toward the ridge. At the far end of the field was a trough. He pointed it out to Kate. "Let's water the horses."

They slowed to a walk, Kate's smile still full. "This is incredible. Tempest, you're such a good girl!" She leaned forward and patted her horse. "Thank you!" She was slightly out of breath.

They slid off the horses, and both Tempest and Champ made their way to the water. Dylan stepped over to the fence, and Kate stepped up on the lower rail. "Just look at all this."

The sun was low in the sky. They probably had a couple hours before twilight would descend on them. A nice breeze had picked up. The late crop in the west field shifted with the wind, and the amber tips flowed like water across the rolling expanse. He breathed deeply and was filled with a supreme contentment. He reached for Kate's hand and then pulled her into his arms. "I like you here."

She melted into him, her arms encircling his back. "I like me here too." She stepped back enough that she could look up into his face.

Softly, gently he pressed his lips to hers.

It was meant to be a simple thing, an appreciation for them

being together, but the minute his mouth touched her soft lips, he was captured by a beautiful longing. He kissed her again, and then again. Each kiss not enough, each kiss ending with the hope for more. Until he gave up keeping it simple and pressed his lips to hers with more urgency, asking, hoping, pleading.

He wanted Kate in his life. The more he knew her, the more clear that became. Her hands went up into his hair, showering sensations through him. He clutched at her back and moved her up against the fence. She pressed into him. He pulled her close and was lost. Lost to the call of his land, to the beauty of the woman in his arms, and to the sense that he wanted her there, with him, always.

More and more he kissed her, held her, cared for her, until a soft nudge at his arm broke into his thoughts, a gentle nicker.

Kate's lips smiled and broke the magic of their kiss, but he smiled back and they laughed together, close, lips still moving over one another. "Hello, Champ," he murmured against her mouth.

The sound of approaching hooves surprised him, though. He lifted his head and immediately recognized a lone figure moving toward them in a blur. "Shelby."

"What?" Kate's head jerked around, and then she turned to him again. A flash of guilt, insecurity, and resignation all moved across her face, and he wanted to erase each one of those feelings.

"Kate."

"No, it is what it is, right?" She shrugged.

"What does that mean?"

"She was here first."

He shook his head. "No. I want you to know this, right now. This is real to me. Obviously I need to work through communicating that to Shelby, but us, I want us." He tried to let her see, to show her his sincerity.

She studied him and then nodded. "But she's my roommate."

He sighed. "Yeah. I'll take care of letting her know. Kate, she has completely ignored me for over a year."

"I know. She's..." Kate shook her head then stood taller. "She's dating, too, you know."

"Which gives her no right to think anything about us."

"Well, there's sort of a code. You know, don't date your roommate's ex..."

Shelby was almost there. He could see her determined expression. "Hey, let's get back up on the horses. Maybe she's just passing through."

Kate shrugged. "Maybe."

The disappointment between them was real. And whatever magic had been there moments ago was gone.

As soon as they were up on their horses, Shelby approached. She was in full riding gear, and Dylan groaned inside. She was showing off. She leapt over the fence behind them and then pulled to a stop at the water trough. "Wow! I miss being up on a horse. This land, these paths." She grinned. "You taking Kate up to the ridge?" She turned to Kate. "It's our favorite lookout point." The dreamy look in her eyes might have given him hope six months ago, but now he only wished she'd tone it down.

"Hey, Shelby. Out for a ride?" Dylan reached out his knuckles for a fist bump.

"Well, yeah. I saw you guys riding across the fields. I didn't want to miss this. It's been at least a year since I've seen the sunset from up there." Her meaningful look was not lost on Dylan or Kate, either. She stiffened and moved her horse to the side.

"Maybe we need to get going, then?" Kate looked from Dylan to Shelby and back.

Kate pulled out to the front even though she was the only one who'd never been there, and Shelby rode at his side. No.

This was not going to happen. He turned to Shelby and lifted his hands. "What are you doing?"

"I told you. I didn't want to miss this. If you're gonna show Kate all our favorite spots, I want to show her too. She's my roommate." She blinked innocently at him, and he knew it was a sham.

"And?"

"And…" Her lower lip appeared. "I didn't want to miss being up here with you, Dylie. Being back home, out here on the land, on the ridge." The sorrow that filled her eyes was real, and his heart went out to her.

"I know, Bee. I've been feeling like that for over a year now."

"I'm sorry. I didn't understand. I think I just needed to see what it's like out there, to experience things."

"Hmm."

"And now I know the best part of my life is all right here." She tried to reach a hand over to him, but he shifted.

"We need to talk."

"Oh, we don't need to change anything or have some big talk. I just wanted you to know. I appreciate us." The sincerity in her face touched him. Maybe she wasn't trying to get him back. Maybe she was just being friendly. He nodded, wary but hopeful.

He nudged his horse forward and joined Kate.

She was a closed book to him now. Her small smile was friendly but nothing more. Shelby might claim to be friendly, but her presence had changed the whole dynamic, and now he was riding up to the ridge with his ex-girlfriend and new… interest? He wished he could call Kate his girlfriend. But the presence of Shelby just proved that he had some things to work out in his life before he could move forward with Kate.

Shelby huffed. "Oh, this is not gonna do. Dylie, this is not how we do the ridge."

Kate almost rolled her eyes. He saw it, and he wanted to do

something, say something to help ease her way with this most awkward of all situations.

But she surprised him. She turned to Shelby. "How do you usually do the ridge? I'm game."

"Oh, I don't know if it's wise to ride the way we usually do. You're new in the saddle."

"I think I can handle it."

"Well, if you say so."

Before Dylan could do anything, Shelby leapt forward on her horse and tore through the trees toward the steep incline.

"Kate," Dylan warned.

But she ignored him or didn't hear him, and she soon tore after Shelby.

Watching her ride, dodging low-lying branches, Dylan had to hand it to her. For never really riding, she had an excellent seat.

He had no choice but to follow the two of them as they raced up to the ridge. He whipped out his phone and took a picture just to show Decker. Maybe he'd have some advice for him. Or better yet, his mama.

Their laughter up ahead was encouraging. He followed, Champ knowing the way even in the growing dark, and soon he'd caught up so he was close enough to hear their conversation.

"This is the best after dark. I can't tell you how many times we lost track of time, you know." Shelby laughed. "You can imagine. And then we had to ride down, trying to make curfew before he had extra chores. The Dawsons are strict with some things. But the best family in the world."

Kate didn't answer.

Shelby kept on talking. "I remember one time we were stuck up here in a rainstorm. There's this big, beautiful tree. Well, you'll see it. And you stay mostly dry under it. We waited out the storm there. But you could see..." Her voice drifted away as they moved further up the hill. Wow, would Kate ever want to come up here again after every spot of the land was marked with a Shelby memory? Would she want to still try to make things work at all? He didn't know. But he hoped this weekend he could try to see where this would go.

CHAPTER 18

ate kept up with Shelby and her race up the mountain. It felt like a mountain to her, steep and rocky, though it was probably more of a hill. Tempest seemed to know the way, and Shelby raced over the land like she could do it in her sleep. From the way she talked, Kate was heading to the regular make-out place for her and Dylan.

She gritted her teeth. At least Kate hadn't kissed him at the top of the ridge.

Though that kiss at the fence. That was a life-changing kind of kiss. That was a we're-meant-to-be-together kind of experience. She was pretty sure Dylan had felt it too.

Kate's short experience with Dylan couldn't compete with the history Shelby had with him. And she'd given up trying to compete with Shelby a long time ago. The woman was happiest if she felt like the most important, most talked about, most vital part of any situation. As soon as conversation shifted elsewhere, she tiresomely brought it back. It became much easier just to talk to and about her.

Sadly, that's what this ride had become. Another Shelby show.

Tempest's hooves slid. "Whoa girl."

"Slow down, Kate," Dylan yelled.

Shelby called back. "Totally. Don't feel like you have to try and keep up."

That was enough to egg her on. She tapped Tempest's flank with her heels. The horse sped up, almost riding into the back of Shelby's horse.

"We take it easy on this part." Shelby called back over her shoulder.

"Why?" Kate lunged past her. "Don't go slow on my account." She urged Tempest up and around Shelby.

But the shale was slippery. And jumping off the trail put her and the horse in the middle of it. Her hooves started to slide more. Tempest stumbled, sliding more and more down the incline, down past Shelby, who watched with open-mouthed concern, and past Dylan, who looked like he was going to dive after her. But then she found her footing again, stumbled around a bit off-trail and made her way to the path behind Dylan.

Kate caught her breath, and so did Tempest. Kate's hand on the side of her head was an apology. "You take it from here, girl."

They started moving again but at a slower pace. Kate let Shelby race up the rest of the way, and she just plodded along. This life was Shelby's anyway. She'd been born here, had ridden her whole life, and had dated Dylan all through high school. Kate was kidding herself if she thought she could just fit right in and make something of herself as a rancher. She laughed. She was a New York agent. And she was happy with that.

Dylan stayed close to her. He didn't say anything, just rode along in front. Kate could tell by the turn of his head how aware he was of her every move. He probably wished he could run like Shelby had. He probably wished he was up there with Shelby. The sun started to set behind them, but she kept plodding along. They were going to miss the sunset. She sighed.

"This next part is easy again." Dylan called back over his shoulder. And Tempest picked up the pace again to follow Champ. Kate just let the horse lead the way. She had already made enough of a mistake for one ride. She could have hurt the horse, broken her ankle. She could have fallen. Why did she think she could pretend she knew anything about horses?

They arrived at the top almost together. Dylan reached for her hand and then tugged.

"What?"

He maneuvered and lifted her so quickly she was not expecting it at all. She found herself sitting with him in his saddle, facing the setting sun.

His breath in her ear tingled through her. "This is better."

She smiled.

He rode out to the edge, and they watched together as the sun slid below the horizon. His arms wrapped around her, and for a moment, she pretended like they were the only two people at the top of the ridge. He whispered, "This right here is going to be my favorite memory up here."

She nodded.

He nuzzled her neck, kissing her just below the earlobe, and then Shelby's voice jarred them.

"Are you not coming all the way up?" Her head peered over the top of an outcropping of rock. "Oh, stopping down there? That's cool. This is a little bit of a rough go. It was beautiful, though. I thought of Prom." She giggled. "And all that." Her head disappeared again, and Kate's shoulders slumped.

"I'm really sorry about this." His words were a balm, and she clung to them in reassurance.

"Like I said. I'm in a bit of a spot."

"We will get this all figured out."

Kate nodded, but she wasn't sure how they could. "This is nice, though." She leaned back against him, and they watched the last of the glow in the sky dim and the colors shift as the day turned to night.

Tempest huffed a breath.

Kate whispered her next fear, "How do we get down in the dark?" She didn't want to go off the trail again and hit that shale. She wasn't sure what to do in the dark on a horse. Did she guide it?

"I'd like to keep you right here with me." His lips ran kisses along the scoop of her neck, and she knew she would deny him nothing.

He paused. "Will that work for you?" His lips smiled against her skin and she made more of her neck available by tilting her head.

"I can't tell. Do that again."

He laughed and then nipped her neck with his teeth. "You are trouble, Kate Reece."

"The good kind?"

"The very best." He held her closer and rested his chin on her shoulder. "But I think it's time to head back."

As if on cue, Shelby came down around the rock outcropping. "We ready?" She didn't look at them. Kate couldn't tell what she was thinking or see her expression in the dark. But Dylan just nudged his horse forward, and they followed Shelby. Tempest fell in behind.

"What a good horse."

"They know to follow. We train most of our own horses. Decker actually does a lot of that."

"Really! Do you think he'd let me watch?"

"Sure. Let's ask him what he has on the schedule. Maybe nothing, but even so, he can bring one of the younger guys out and show you a few things."

She nodded. "I'd like that."

They made it down and separated from Shelby at the watering trough. Kate could have ridden her own horse at this point. The stars were bright, the moon was coming out, and the trail was visible. But she stayed put, and Dylan didn't say anything about moving her.

They didn't say anything. She was lost in thought. They were almost to the house when Dylan spoke. "I'm sorry about Shelby."

She sighed and leaned more of her weight against him. "I know."

"But I'm grateful for her, too."

"Why's that?"

"Cause if it wasn't for her, I would have never met you."

She smiled into the darkness. "That's true." In her mind, it didn't necessarily make it the best move on her part. Though it wasn't her fault that she and Dylan had connected so easily and quickly. She'd run into him before she even knew he *was* Dylan. She sighed again. "I don't know much about this, but I do know I'm glad I met you and I'm super grateful for this weekend."

He nuzzled her again. "Me too." They arrived at the barn gate. He got off, opened it, led them in, and closed it behind. His hands reached up and cupped her hips at each side. Then he lowered her to the ground so she stood right in front of him. Right where she wanted to be. She stood up on her toes, horse behind, Dylan in front, and found his lips on their way to meet her own.

The kiss was soft, sure, and full of promises. But too short. He clucked, and the horses followed. "I'll take care of these two. You want to head on into the house? I bet Mama has something for us in the kitchen."

"Okay, great." She made her way to the side door. Did they use the side door? When she tried it, it opened, so she stepped inside to a full workroom, it looked like. It was almost a garage from the looks of all the things they stored in there. She imagined not many people ever used this door. She made her way to the other side of the room, where she saw a dim light and another door.

But she stopped partway into the room. Mama sat there at a cluttered desk, with her head in her hands. Kate tried to tiptoe back out the way she'd come, but the dear woman turned. "Come on in, sweet lady. I'm just living a few memories worth remembering." Her eyes were tired and sad, but light twinkled in their depths.

She approached slowly. "I'm so sorry to disturb you. Dylan said to come on in, but he never told me which door…"

Mama shook her head. "Don't you worry about that. Come, tell me about your ride."

Kate sat in the chair right next to Mama. The desk was full of rodeo things. Belt buckles, medals, ribbons, as well as paperwork and an old horseshoe, even a nail. This definitely didn't look much like a woman's work desk. "It was beautiful up there."

"And my Dylan? He was a gentleman?"

"Oh, of course. You've raised such a good man in Dylan. All your boys seem to be perfectly honorable and good men."

"Yes, they are. We're mighty proud of them." She lifted a small framed photograph of her and a tall man, broad in the shoulders, as broad as any of his sons. He had his arm around her, and the two of them looked as happy as Kate had ever seen a couple.

"Mr. Dawson?"

She nodded. "He was a good man, their father. If he were here, half of the troubles we ever find ourselves in around this place wouldn't even be a bother." She sighed. "That Shelby would have been gone years ago."

Kate gasped. "Really!"

"Oh yes, honey. She's got her ropes around Dylan in ways not one of us has been able to untangle. Until you."

"She was up there with us."

"On the ridge?"

"Yes."

Mama shook her head. "You hold your ground, Kate. Don't let her womanly sneaks do anything to change what you want."

Kate smiled. "I don't even know what I want."

Her eyes searched Kate's. "Oh, I think you do. You're just not sure how to go about it."

Kate opened her mouth and then closed it and nodded. "That's exactly right."

She winked. "This old mama knows a thing or two."

"I've heard that, and now I see it's true."

Mama patted her hand. "Well, I'm happy you've come to stay with us. I see a lot of good in you. I bet you get a lot of really good books out into this world. Heaven knows we need it."

Kate tipped her head. She wasn't sure how much good the books were doing in the world. They were certainly sure to sell a bunch of copies, but really, Kate had yet to find one that she thought would really make its mark in a good way. "I'm trying. I'll tell you that much." She knew now she would try even harder. "Books are important. They change lives."

Mama reached up to pull down a thick and worn Bible. "They surely do."

"And that right there is my favorite book of all."

"This is Mr. Dawson's copy. He used to mark it up like crazy. I don't like coloring in mine. I like to learn a new thing every time instead of the same thing over and over."

"I've never thought of it like that."

"Dylan marks up a new one every now and then." She shook her head fondly. "That boy is a real good mix of me and his father."

Kate could only hope that was true, for she was already seeing a lot to admire in the woman at her side.

"One of his favorite verses I know you've heard before. But it bears remembering because as soon as you know you're on

God's path for you, you just hold on and trust and stick to that path. It will work out. The whys and the hows and the particulars all fall into place." She opened up to Proverbs. "Trust in the Lord with all your heart. And lean not unto thine own understanding. In all thy ways acknowledge him, and he shall direct thy paths."

Kate sighed, this time in happy, peaceful recognition. "One of my very favorites. I read that right before I moved out to New York."

"And they'll help you again now as you're trying to make your way. I know the Lord is with us. He's in the details, mark my words, and He is surely hoping you and my son make something beautiful together."

Kate's mouth opened and her face heated, but she couldn't help but love this woman. "Thank you, Mama Dawson." She reached out and gave her a squeeze across the shoulders.

"Now, I was hoping you'd call me that." She grinned. "Let's get you in the house with a cup of the famous Dawson hot cocoa."

"Oh, I bet this is gonna be good."

"You'll never want another after." She stood, leaning on the desk a little bit to right herself and then led the way through the door and into a well-lit hall.

"The kitchen's just up ahead here."

Dylan stepped into their line of sight.

"Now don't you go worrying. I've had her in Dad's office."

"Really?" Dylan looked curiously from one to the other.

Kate blushed. "I entered the house through the outside door in there, I guess."

"And I've been sharing God's word with her just like Father used to do with you."

"Sounds about right to me. Mama, Kate reads her Bible all the time."

"She rubbing off on you in that regard?"

He considered them both and then nodded. "She is." He reached for Kate's hand. "Since we talked, I've been reading every day."

"That's my girl." Mama smiled at Kate. "Now let's get some cookies out to go with our hot cocoa."

Kate laughed. "I don't know why all the Dawsons don't just live here forever."

"Mama wonders that same thing." Dylan laughed. "I'm just glad we are training here in San Antonio. Just wait till you have Sunday dinner."

"I think I'm gonna love it."

Dylan nodded.

Although nothing was really working out the way she'd imagined, and she didn't know if she and Dylan could ever progress to much of anything, she had been reminded that God was in the details. If she trusted, things had a way of finding their way home.

CHAPTER 19

*D*ylan, Kate, and his mama had sat together for long hours last night, so long that now, on his five a.m. drive back to the fairgrounds, he was really struggling to keep his eyes open. But he would never regret it. Where Shelby had made a mess of things, his Kate and his mama had made them clear.

Kate seemed certain of something. If not their future, of herself. Or more, she seemed certain of God's hand. And that was just what they both needed. Things would work out. God would help them. And they could move forward with the little knowledge they had.

He exhaled long and slow. He sure hoped the path would open up sooner rather than later. God's time was a tricky thing. Did he really want to wait?

But in the meantime, he had a rodeo to win. He was working on his speed. They'd discovered a tweak to his technique that could trim off even the tiniest fraction of a second. It was worth it. The world champions were sometimes just off from each other by that much time. Or that much presentation.

Today would be busy and repetitive, and practice could be

grueling for him and Pepper, but at least he would have thoughts of Kate to keep him company.

Partway into the day, he was really pushing and struggling and not improving. Scooter stood by with the hose to keep Pepper from overheating. Even though they were moving into late October, the days were still hot sometimes, but the nights were blessedly cool. He drank long and deep from his water bottle.

"Hey, cowboy." Kate's voice felt like the cool drink sliding down his throat.

"Oh, wow I'm glad to see you." He wiped his forehead and adjusted his hat. "But I'm a mess."

Her eyes traveled over his tight shirt, wet through with sweat, his jeans, his boots, his hat. She took so long checking him out he had to laugh. But then she just said, "You look just right to me."

He tipped his hat. "What you got there?"

"I brought us some lunch. Us if you have time to eat with me, or if not, it's just for you."

"Now that's just what a man likes to hear." He turned to Scooter on the opposite fence. "We're taking a break. Can you give Pepper all kinds of pampering for me?"

"Sure thing, boss."

Kate swung down from the fence. "You the boss around here?"

"Boss to some, peon to others." He grabbed a cooled towel off the fence railing, wiping down his face. "Do you mind if I spray off a little?"

She laughed. "Go right ahead. I can help if you want."

He eyed her, the raised eyebrow, the daring in her face. "You sure you want to go there?"

"Oh, I've never been more sure." She took off the light shirt hanging loose over her tank top and tucked that in. "Now, where's this hose?"

He took in the sight of her—shorts, boots, white tank—and his grin grew. "My lunch just got a whole lot more enjoyable."

She laughed. "Don't be too sure of that." She stretched her hands above her head.

He headed over to where a hose and spicket were coiled up in the dirt. He moved slowly, hoping she wouldn't notice it, but then she raced past.

"Aha!" She grabbed the hose and turned it toward him, her hand on the lever. "Where were you wanting to get cooled off?"

He held out his hands. "You pick a place. Hose me down."

She laughed. "You sure about this?"

"Absolutely. Little lady, clean off your man so he's presentable for lunch."

"Oh I like the sound of that." She turned on the hose and let him have it. His shirt, his arms, even his head. He dipped so she could let the water cascade all over the back of his head and neck, and then while she was standing real close, he snatched the hose and did the same to her.

She screamed and tried to get it back, and they ended up wrestling for it on the grass. With blades of grass sticking to them, their clothes wet through, he held up his hands. "Mercy! Uncle! What do you say? I give!"

She laughed and started to spray herself off.

Watching her for a minute, he reached out a hand. "If I promise to be nice, can I help?"

She nodded.

He pulled her to her feet and sent the water over her back, catching all the grass, and letting it drain down her front and then down her legs. Her boots had long since been discarded, and her bright blue toes blinked up at him. "I like your pedicure."

"You got me addicted."

"As it should be." He handed her the hose, and she did the same for him until they were drenched through and grass free.

He shook his hair. "Now, did that lunch come from my mama's kitchen?"

"It did, but I made it."

"Even better." He led her to a log sitting in the hot sun. "I think I'm ready to bake a little."

She shivered. "Yeah, that sun feels real nice now."

They pulled out sandwiches. He checked inside. "Now, this is some sandwich!"

"My favorite kind."

"I feel like I'm in a New York Deli."

They each ate, with large bites, their full and overflowing roast beef sandwiches.

His boss rounded the corner. "Dylan!"

Dylan sat up and swallowed his sandwich, lifting a hand, but Boss didn't see him.

"Dylan! Shelby said she's coming over with lunch." He stopped. "Oh, hey. Looks like you got lunch taken care of."

"Yeah. I'll be back at it when she gets here, probably."

He nodded, watching the two of them.

"Hey, Trev, This is Kate Reece."

"Nice to meet you, Kate." He tipped his hat. "Glad to see someone's taking care of our star here."

"Doing my best, sir."

"She's visiting this weekend then she has to head back to New York. But if you can get her to stay, I'd be much obliged."

"Well, now, I'll do my best." Trev eyed the two of them again with a small shake of his head and then went back to where he'd come from.

"Does Shelby always bring lunch?"

"What? Nah." She had back in the day. The guys who'd been around back then had looked forward to Shelby's lunches.

"Should I have brought food for everyone?"

He shook his head. "Nope. You did exactly what you

shoulda, which was whatever you wanted. And I appreciate it." He kissed her forehead. "Thank you."

"You're welcome."

"And now you're gonna be soaking wet going home. Here, come on. I'll get you some dry clothes." He stood and picked up her boots and took her hand.

She whistled, an exact mimic of his.

"Where did you learn to do that?"

She laughed as Sammy came running. "Sam!" She crouched down, and his dog nearly knocked her over. "Who's a good boy? Who's my Sammy!" He licked her face, and then Dylan pushed him away. "Down."

He held the door open for her and followed her up into his trailer.

"Wow, it's so clean."

"And she's surprised." He shook his head.

"I'm teasing. No Dawson brother would have a messy trailer."

"Now, I'm not saying anything about Nash or Decker. But, me, I'm clean." He opened the fridge. "Want something to drink?"

"Yes. Even though I just got doused, my mouth is dry."

He handed her a water bottle and then shuffled through his drawers. "I don't think I have anything you won't drown in, but maybe drawstring sweats?"

"Perfect." She smiled. "And a sweatshirt?"

He nodded, secretly pleased she was liking the idea of wearing his clothes. He handed her a towel from the cabinet above his tiny shower and then a stack of clothes. "You can change in there."

She scooted past him, but his hands on her hips stopped her. He pulled her close. "Thanks for lunch." Her lips were cold against his warm mouth, and he wanted to linger there a moment, but then he stopped, resisted tapping her on the backside, and turned to find his own dry clothes.

"You're welcome." She shut the door to his bedroom.

Man, it was nice having her in there with him. What would it be like to travel, to do shows, if she was always there with him? He'd always thought Shelby would do that with him. She was more the type, he guessed. She fit in with all the guys, hung out with the extra hands when he wasn't around, flirted with the world, but kissed only him.

He shook his head. But Kate was not like Shelby, and he was glad for that. Kate had a life, dreams, hopes. Well, like they said, they were gonna live day to day before they tried to figure out the hows of later.

When she came out, all wrapped up in his clothes, he wanted nothing more than to push her right back to his bed and kiss her until she was heavy-lidded and cozy, but he knew now was not the time. As they moved down the stairs to exit his trailer, he turned. "There's only one thing that's making me leave this trailer with you looking as good as you do, and that's my mama."

She choked. "Your mama?"

He nodded. "No way would she have me doing all the things I want to do with you and still go to church on Sunday."

He turned before he could see the deep red he knew filled her face. Man, she was fun to tease. Truth is, he was grateful she was just as good a woman as his mama, and even if he knew she enjoyed his kisses, she knew when they were appropriate and when to stop. And that's something he never had with Shelby. He shook his head. He needed to stop comparing the women. They were different, in almost every way.

Shelby pulled up in a bright red Jeep.

"Is that her car?" Kate stood beside him, her wet clothes in hand.

"Yep."

"You need me here?"

"Always." He tapped her nose. "But if you have to get back to work, that's fine too."

"I've half a mind to stick around."

He scooped her up and held her close. "You feeling possessive?"

"Maybe."

"I like that." He kissed her and then placed her back on her feet. "Oh, and don't forget your boots." He reached down by his door and handed them to her. "Wait. I'll just carry you." He turned and offered his back. She jumped up, and he held her and the boots all the way to her car.

They passed Shelby. She, for once, was at a complete loss, or at least it looked that way. "Hey, Shelby. You sticking around?" Dylan asked.

"For a minute."

Kate climbed in the driver's seat, and Dylan watched her until the car turned out of sight.

He knew Shelby stood beside him before he saw her. She seemed quiet.

"She's wearing your sweatshirt."

He didn't answer.

"That the one I used to wear?"

He shook his head. "Nope. I think you burned it."

"I did not!"

His laugh made her smile. "Come on. You don't even care. You haven't talked to me in over a year."

"I might care, though. What if I cared?" Her eyes, full of questions, didn't tug at his heart the way Kate's did.

"Then you'd tell me, I'm sure."

"And then?"

"And then what? Shelby, you've had a long time to come back, and you don't want to. We both know it." He stopped short of telling her he wouldn't take her anyway. He wasn't sure

156

what held his tongue, but it seemed unreasonably cruel at this point. If they could both leave happily not chasing the other, things would be better.

She turned from him without another word. "Boss!"

"Yep!" Trev answered from somewhere across the arena.

"I got lunch."

"Bless! You hear that? Shelby's got lunch!"

The guys gathered, and Dylan was glad of it. But he headed back to Pepper. He picked up his ropes, climbed up into the saddle and ran through his routine. When he was done, Scooter held up the stopwatch. "You did it! Record time. Keep doing that and you got yourself an Olympic offer!"

He nodded. Yep. Life was sure better when Kate was a part of it. He just didn't know how he could keep her close.

CHAPTER 20

*K*ate hated to leave knowing Shelby was there, unloading lunch for all the guys, winning them all over, but she had work to do. And she'd promised Mama she'd help with the flowers. So she drove back, drinking in the smell of Dylan's sweatshirt, knowing she was doing the right thing but sort of hating it the whole way.

Her phone dinged. Text from Dylan. "I just had my best time roping ever. You're good for me, woman."

She pulled over. "I always knew I was meant to have a cowboy in my life." She sent a heart emoji and then said, "You're good for me too." She clicked a selfie and sent it. Too much? She didn't care. Still heady from her time in his trailer, she felt like she could stand on top of the world and not be winded. And besides, for all she knew, Shelby was standing right there watching him receive his texts.

Her groan was full of frustration and disappointment but, oddly, also hope and longing. Wow, she was an emotion salad.

When she pulled up in front of the Dawson home, Mama Dawson was already out in front, digging around by the mums. Kate parked and hopped out. "I'm here. Let's get this done."

"Oh, honey, good to see you. I know you were doing more important things, taking care of my son."

She smiled. "Or he was taking care of me, I don't know." She laughed at her sweatshirt.

"Well, you look cute. Come on down here. I'll show you what we need to do. And then you get inside and get your work done. I don't want to keep you from that."

"No problem. This is more important anyway."

They dug and planted and transferred flowers. Kate finally gave voice to the thoughts that circled through her head. "I was thinking about what we talked about."

"About trusting God."

"Mm-hmm. I trust Him. I always have. But I'm thinking maybe I don't trust Him enough to walk away, or to take that first step or whatever. I trust Him enough to let things happen to me, but not to be the one doing the action, making the decisions. That's me, just waiting for life to happen, trusting that it's all according to God's plan."

"And how has that worked for you?"

"Honestly, really great."

"Then what's the problem?"

"Sometimes I think we have to do something too, you know? I don't know. Just something I thought. Today, I went to take Dylan some lunch. And it was great. We talked and got in a water fight." She laughed, not believing she was talking about this with Dylan's mother. "But then Shelby showed up." She shrugged. "I couldn't just stay there trying to keep his attention, or the team's attention, you know?"

"Of course not. You have self-respect." She nodded.

"Thank you." Kate leaned over and gave her a gentle squeeze across the shoulders. "So that was time to walk away, to walk away and trust. Just 'cause Shelby's there doesn't mean I'm gonna lose him or she's gonna get him. It just means I have work to do and flowers to plant. And it's in God's hands."

"That's my girl." She wiped her forehead. "I think you got something there." She tucked the last flower in the last hole. "Now, I'm gonna water these. Thank you for your help. You get yourself some work done. 'Cause tonight is some more fun around here, and tomorrow is Sunday dinner."

"I'll be ready. Thank you for letting me help you do the flowers."

"Thank you, darling. Now every time I see them, I'll think of you."

Kate nodded, wiped her hands off on a small towel they'd carried with them, and entered the house.

Once her hands were washed, her laptop open, and the emails coming in, she centered herself on work. She went through them one at a time, almost by rote at this point, until the next one dinged in. It was from a huge publishing house. She clicked it open and then jumped in the air, squealing. Immediately, she picked up her phone.

One of her author's picked up.

"I have news. Are you sitting down? Penwich Publishing wants your book. They want it bad."

The screams on the other end of the phone were even more happy than her own.

They talked about what would happen next, and Kate made plans to go to lunch with the editor assigned to the project. This would make her career. One big sale like this would put her on the map. This was the start of everything.

She stood and moved to stare out the window. Land stretched in every direction. It really was a beautiful place. New York was beautiful too, in its own way. The people, the pace, the buildings. She really loved it there. And now... She breathed in deeply. Now her career was taking off. Dylan would be travelling everywhere, from one city to another, for a couple years at least. It really wasn't time for her to be with him anyway. So going straight back to New York to work with this new client and grow her career was important, okay. She wasn't just walking out on the best thing in her life.

She nodded one, twice, again, trying to convince herself.

Either way, she was leaving the day after tomorrow. And they would see each other when they could. They would get together when they could, just like they had already. She leaned her forehead against the cold glass and closed her eyes. What she really wanted was to just be with him every day, all day. Which of course, she couldn't do, no matter what

She didn't know what any of this had to do with her conversation with Mama Dawson on trusting in God, but it must be somehow related. She had something to learn here. She sighed, and the window fogged. Well, whatever it was, she would learn it and get to know Dylan by phone as she became a famous and rich agent. She laughed. Maybe not so rich, or famous, but she definitely had a lot to do in New York and nothing whatsoever to do in Texas or on tour with the rodeo. So that was that.

She called her boss. "Hey, Juliene. I got a book deal with Penwich Publishing."

"You don't have it yet."

"But they sent an email."

"They are sending out feelers. You don't have it until they sign."

"So what do I do?"

"You get back here and write a contract they are gonna sign."

She nodded. "Okay. The conference…"

"Don't worry about that. We'll meet Sunday, and you can get with the client and the publisher Monday."

"Okay. Right."

"Good work, Kate. Welcome to the big time."

"Thanks."

She hung up and suddenly didn't feel as happy as she had moments before. Sunday dinner. She was going to miss the Dawson Sunday dinner if she left.

She laughed at her own ridiculous thoughts, give up the best thing to happen to her career for a Sunday dinner?

A quick search pulled up three flights she could take the next day that would get her home in enough time for an evening meeting with her boss. The last one left at five. She reserved it.

Then she went in search of Mama Dawson to tell her the change of plans.

But when she told her she was missing Sunday dinner, Mama shook her head. "Then we'll just move Sunday dinner."

"What? I thought it was sacred. Sunday dinner. The whole family." She didn't want the Dawsons to change everything around for her.

"It doesn't matter what day we have it. You're worth it. I'll just tell Decker to let everyone know."

She squeezed Mama tightly. "Thank you."

"Oh you're welcome, darling."

They moved downstairs together. Decker stepped out into the hallway.

"Oh good. Decker, tell your brothers we're having Sunday dinner today."

"Today? I don't know. They might have plans."

"Tell them to cancel them. It's Saturday this week. Kate has to head back to New York."

Kate tried to look apologetic, but she was too pleased to feel too sorry.

"In that case, we better move it all to Saturday."

Kate laughed. "Thank you." She shrugged. "It's okay if not everyone can make it."

Decker shook his head.

"No, it isn't. It's never okay if they can't make it. If you don't come, you call in." Mama placed a hand on Kate's forearm. "You're welcome to call in too if you like."

"Thank you."

The kitchen became a whirlwind. Kate stood at Mama's side,

throwing things together. She was amazed at how much food they were cooking and how quickly. "You'll be just as good," Mama reassured her, "don't you worry."

Bailey stepped in to join them. "Did I hear something about Sunday dinner on a Saturday?" She kissed Mama's cheek. "Kate, you must be one special lady."

"Of course she is."

"I'm here to help."

After more chopping and baking and stirring than Kate had ever done, dinner was cooking, and they were resting. They sat at the kitchen table, delicious smells starting to come from all around them.

Kate sighed. "Wow, that was a lot of work."

"It sure was, honey, but it's worth it. Just wait till you see everyone together. Just wait till you see their faces and hear them razzing each other. It's a beautiful thing for a mama to see."

She reached a hand out to take Mama's in her own. "Thank you for sharing it with me."

"Of course. You're real special. I can tell. And I know Dylan thinks so too."

The door opened, and in walked Dylan with Shelby right behind him. "Did we hear something about Sunday dinner being on Saturday?" He swooped in, kissed his mama, and then kissed Kate.

Bailey's eyes went wide, and she winked.

Shelby seemed perfectly fine about it, though she was standing overly close to Dylan.

"Do you care if I come too? I haven't had a Dawson Sunday dinner in years."

"Of course you can come." Mama stood. "Now's a good time to get that table set, isn't it?"

"I'll do that for you, Mama." Dylan moved toward the cabinets.

"I'll help." Shelby moved to join him. "Has anyone called Nash?"

"Multiple times," Decker called from the other room. "Want to see if you can get him?"

"Yep. On it." She put the phone to her ear.

Everyone started moving plates and forks and cups out to the dining room. Kate watched as Shelby dug a tablecloth out of the cabinet and spread it on the large table. Suddenly she felt like a very foreign, distant part of the family. And that was okay. She had just met them all. But for a brief moment, she'd felt closer.

"Nash is coming!"

"Oh, well done, Shelby." Mama nodded in her direction.

Kate stood. "I think I'll go take a minute." No one in particular heard or answered, and she really didn't know who she was talking to. So she moved slowly out of the room and found a place on the front porch swing. With one leg dangling down to kick off a little swinging motion, she moved back and forth while she thought things through.

What if the timing was all off? What if she had things to do in New York and he had a rodeo to complete and a girlfriend to figure out?

If she and Dylan were together now, it would just make things more difficult.

His laugh carried out onto the porch. She was going to miss that laugh.

A loud car horn sounded out across the front yard. Nash. She smiled. Grace came around from the side of the house, hand in hand with Maverick.

"I hear you're the guest of honor to a one-time-only Sunday dinner on a Saturday?"

"You heard right." She smiled.

Then Shelby's laugh carried outside.

"And we have an interloper." Maverick winked. "Is that why you're out here?"

"She fits in so well. She even knows where the tablecloths are."

"That is a sign of a good marriage."

"Maybe it is." She looked away.

"Come on. I'm just teasing. Look, I'll send Dylan out here to show you what's what about who he wants to be with."

"No, don't worry about it. I'm coming back inside."

"I could send you two out to the barn to watch the moonrise if you want. That seemed to work pretty well on Bailey."

"That sounds nice."

They moved into the house just as the last of the table was being set. Nash stepped in right behind them.

"And now we're all here." Mama moved to her place at the table. And everyone else seemed to find a place, including Shelby and Dylan. But someone had left a spot open on the other side of Dylan. His eyes found hers, and the smile he gave her about melted her insides with happiness. It was full and heartfelt. He patted the seat beside him.

She hurried to sit and everyone joined hands.

Mama looked at her. "Kate, would you say it?"

"I'd be honored." She bowed her head. What could she say? What words could she say so that God would bless this dear family and that they would know she loved them? "Dear Heavenly Father, we are grateful to be gathered together here at this beautiful table with this beautiful family, and we are thankful for thy care. We are thankful Dylan is so successful and that Maverick and Bailey are having another child. We're thankful Decker is helping so much here at home and that Nash is here with us for dinner even at the last minute. We are thankful for dear Grace also. And for Shelby. Please bless Mama. And bless this dear family." Dylan squeezed her hand. She kept going. Turned out she had much to be grateful for when it came to the Dawsons. She wasn't sure what kinds of prayers they were used to, but this was a long one. But then, just as she was finishing up, the front door burst open and a man ran in, frantic and deeply emotional.

"Daddy! What is it?" Shelby stood up, panic filling her face.

"It's your mother. Come. We must get you to the hospital."

"Oh no! Oh no, no, no!" Shelby clutched her stomach. Her hands started shaking, and she looked like she might pass out.

"Dylan." Mama stood.

He jumped to help and led her to the door where her father waited, anxious to leave.

Dylan asked, "Can I drive you two to the hospital?"

"Yes, thank you, son."

The rest of the Dawsons jumped up, but Mama settled them down. "You all stay put. We have work to do to get some meals going for that family. And you will do no good standing around at the hospital."

They nodded. She spoke sense. It was a very quiet group who finished up the dinner that no one had started. And then Mama put them to work boxing up the rest to send over to Shelby's house.

Eventually Dylan called his mama, who called out the news.

"She had a stroke. It's not looking good. She's in a coma." Mama turned back to the phone. "You stay with her, honey. She needs someone right now." She listened for a moment, then Mama met Kate's eyes and said, "Love you too, son. Bye."

Kate and Bailey cleaned up the dishes.

"Usually the boys do the dishes. It's one of the Dawson rules." Bailey smiled. "But she's got them running food over."

"I'm glad I can do something to help."

They washed and dried in silence for a moment. "So, Maverick knew you in high school, too, didn't he?"

"Yeah, he just kept on loving me even when I was difficult to love."

"So do you think…" She couldn't finish her sentence. Maybe it was the Dawson way. Loyalty and all that.

"I know a lot of us would be happy for Dylan if you two made things work."

Kate nodded.

"But I know what it means to pursue your dreams. And you both have some really great ones going on right now. That's hard to work around."

"Yeah, it really is. I'm working on trusting and hoping and moving forward best I know how."

"What else can you do?" Bailey handed her a plate. "One thing I know about Dawson boys? They never give up on the woman they love."

Kate knew she meant to be supportive, but it was only making her realize that Dylan might never really be hers. What if he still loved Shelby? What if he would be loyal to his first girlfriend just like Maverick had been loyal to Bailey.

"I guess we'll see. Long distance is hard. I'll be going back to New York tomorrow."

They finished cleaning up, and Kate said goodnight and went to bed.

She lay there for an hour, staring at nothing, before she threw back the covers and got out a notepad. Goodbyes were hard for her. She'd make this as easy as possible.

After two notes were written, she fell asleep with her alarm set for early in the morning. She might as well take the first flight out.

CHAPTER 21

$\mathcal{T}$he news about Shelby's mother just kept getting worse. Shelby clung to Dylan as her only support, and Dylan prayed her mother would recover. Shelby's father paced, his face haggard. He only half responded when people talked to him.

But as the night went on with no improvement, Dylan began to wonder if perhaps it was her time to go. Shelby would not take that well.

They sat in the hospital chairs, side by side, far away from the television. Shelby rested her head on his shoulder. He thought she was asleep. And he wondered if he should keep praying or start to prepare her for the worst, or both. Where did faith play a role here? *Trust in the Lord with all thine heart.* The words came to his mind quietly and clearly. Trust. Come what may, trust.

"I had a boyfriend."

"What?" Dylan tried to look down into Shelby's face.

"Ramon. He was my boyfriend—even when you were visiting New York."

He wasn't even irritated with her confession. He would have

been two months ago, but now, it just seemed like a Shelby thing to do. He had Kate. "Okay. Is he a great guy?"

She nodded. "But he broke up with me." Her tears started up anew. And he handed her a tissue.

"Was it because I was there?"

"No, but I think seeing you again showed me that Ramon really isn't that great of a guy." She hiccupped. "I don't know." She sniffed and used the tissue. "But I'm feeling like that's an okay thing. You and I were together for so long, I don't think I know what it's like to be without a boyfriend. Might be good for me to figure out."

"Maybe. And you'll have Kate in New York. You won't be alone. And you'll have me. I'll always be there for you, Shelby." He studied her face. He meant it. She was a good woman. And she didn't deserve to lose her mother. "It was good for me to have that time without a girlfriend, I think."

She nodded. "You're different. A good different." She turned her tear-stained face up to him. "I love you, Dylan. I think I always will."

He wiped her tears. "Maybe like old friends do, but you're gonna find someone who rocks your world, too, and I'll be happy for you."

"Do you ever think we could start over? You and me?"

He considered her for a moment. He had thought that. Even now, the idea had some appeal. Sitting by her, being here for her, helping with her mom, having her at his house, it all felt so normal and natural. She fit right in. New York had been tough, being together there had felt awkward and he'd felt unwanted, but when they were both home, it worked better. Instead of shaking his head no, he just shrugged. "Who knows what could happen."

She put her head back on his shoulder and sighed. "I hope my mama's gonna be okay."

"Me too, Bee." Their hands linked together naturally, and he tried to fill her with any strength he had. Trusting in the Lord meant all kinds of things. It meant accepting when things weren't what you hoped for. It meant working for things you thought were right. It also meant healing and hope for the sick. All they could do was wait and see.

After a full night in the hospital with no news, Dylan convinced Shelby to come on back to his house. Her father was now allowed in the room with her mother, and there was nothing for the two of them to do in the hospital waiting room. With his arm wrapped around her, he moved toward the double doors.

She walked slowly. He remembered what it felt like to lose his dad. At the time, it felt like his world would never be the same. And it hadn't been. "You got this, Shelby. We'll get through it."

She looked up at him, her eyes so desperate, her face lined with sorrow. He pressed his lips to her forehead. "I'm here."

She nodded.

They turned to face the door and a blank-faced Kate. Her eyes flickered to his, but then she rushed to Shelby and pulled her into her arms. "I'm sorry. I'm so sorry."

Shelby started to cry again, but exhaustion had set in, and her tears were soft and quiet. Kate wiped her own eyes. She didn't look at Dylan. "I'm heading to New York right now. So I'll take care of things. You just come on back when you're ready." An Uber waited in front of the hospital.

"You're going now?" Dylan asked.

Kate nodded, only now meeting his gaze fully.

Something was different about her, but he couldn't decipher what it was. Shelby leaned into him again. Kate looked from one to the other and then turned. "Well, bye."

"I'll call you later." Dylan wanted to scoop her up in his arms to seek his own comfort there and let her know she was important, but Shelby felt like she would collapse on the ground if he let go.

Kate waved behind her and hurried to her Uber.

As soon as they got back to his house, Mama took over with Shelby, and Dylan went upstairs to his room for a shower. He pulled his phone out of his pocket to see if Kate had texted. Nothing. But a white envelope rested on his pillow. His eyes felt heavy with exhaustion and he craved a shower, but something told him what that note said. He ripped open the envelope.

Dear Dylan,

I've had an incredible weekend with you and your family. To think I was up on a horse with my own cowboy. I'll never forget the moments we have shared. I got some great news at work which is calling me back, and you have your hands full here. Wish we could have met when less was going on. I'll never forget you.

Kate

A rushed panic rose up inside him. Was this goodbye? It sounded a lot like goodbye. He rang her phone number, and when she didn't answer he tossed the phone on his bed. She was on an airplane. Part of him wanted to head out that door and grab the next flight so they could talk. He sighed. But Shelby's mom was probably dying in the hospital. No matter what, someone had to be here for her.

And he was training for the rodeo. And if Kate said she had to leave for work, then she was probably busy.

A numbness settled over him. There was nothing he could do. He turned on the shower, hoping hot water would wake up his limbs, his mind, his heart. But the only thing he could think right then was "Kate is gone."

After his shower, he went in search of Mama. She was cleaning up whatever she'd just fed Shelby, no doubt. When he stepped into the kitchen, she pulled him into her arms. Then she laughed. "Do you know, sometimes I wish I could still put you on my lap, kiss your finger, and make everything better."

He laughed. "I know, Mama, but your hugs help."

"I hope so, son. Now sit down right here. I have a plate of breakfast."

"Thank you." He tried to enjoy her eggs and hotcakes 'cause they were some of the best in the world, but the numbness had spread to his taste. "Shelby's hurting real bad."

"She sure is. Hopefully she's sleeping. I put her up in Kate's room."

He smiled, small and weak. The idea that Kate had a room in his house made him happy.

"She'll be back," Mama said.

"I don't know. She left me a note that sounded like goodbye."

"It probably was goodbye."

His gaze shot up to her face, hurt hammering through him.

"But don't you worry. She's just putting her trust in the Lord and doing things one step at a time. I have a good feeling about all of this."

"Shelby wants to get back together."

"I'm sure she does. For now."

"You think not forever?"

"Who can tell. We all learn and grow, don't we? I hope she's becoming more the woman I know is inside her." Mama sat down next to him. "You know the Lord doesn't always give us everything we want when we want it. We'd be spoiled to high heaven if that were the case."

Dylan snorted. "Nice, Mom."

"But we are in good hands. We can trust in Him." The fire in her eyes, the definitive nod of her head, and in the way she lived every day of her life testified to her words.

"I know, Mama. It's a hard truth to take when you want something real bad. Look at Shelby. She might lose her mom. We lost Dad. I prayed every day he'd live. And he's gone."

"So did I. And I still sit here sometimes wondering why he's not with us. What's the wisdom in taking such a good man from his family? So many things would be better if he were here." She shook her head with a tiredness he hadn't seen on her face for a long time.

"Maybe you should get some rest too, Mama."

"I will, don't you worry about that. Got plenty of time to rest."

"I know we're in good hands. I know it. But what if Kate doesn't want me, just like Shelby didn't for all that time? What if it's just best to take Shelby for what she is. We can make it work." He dropped his exhausted head into his hands. "I just want to start my family. I'm ready to have someone in my life."

Her hand rested on his back, a solid presence. And something about it felt strong. Words his father often said came into his mind. "You gotta go through the storm before the calm. But don't worry, even in the toughest storm, there is always a calm."

For a minute, her hand felt like two, like his dad was once again resting a hand on his shoulder. And the strength of two worked its way inside. He could almost feel his dad beside him, but when he turned, it was just his mom, with a love in her eyes he knew would never dim. And with her and God, he knew he had what he needed even if Dad was no longer there.

"It doesn't take away the ache, though."

"No, it doesn't." And the truth of those words spoke from her eyes.

"You're a good mother. You've done great by all of us. Thank you for that."

"Of course. When you have your own children, you'll learn of the love for another that cannot be squelched by anything. That's why I know the Lord has this."

He grabbed onto her faith, knowing he'd have to be there for Shelby, train for the rodeo, and figure out his own mess before he'd be ready to make things work with Kate. And even then, nothing would be easy about their long-distance situation. But he would try to do what his mama had told him Kate was doing, move one step at a time in the direction he thought was right and trust God to help take care of the details.

His phone sat silent in his pocket. He just hoped that somewhere in all this, Kate would call him back.

CHAPTER 22

*D*ylan's phone number only responded with ringing for what seemed like forever and then sent her to voicemail. She sighed. Maybe he'd already moved on. His and Shelby's cozy embrace on the way out of the hospital looked so much like a long, well-practiced relationship that she felt even more the outsider in all of this sorrow. But she had been glad to hug Shelby, to let her roommate know Kate was there for her too. And she hoped Shelby's mother would recover, of course.

And now she was coming home from the meeting with her boss all fired up to work out the best deal possible for her client. So she had a lot to distract her from the ache inside, the growing worry that maybe she'd lose Dylan and that trusting things would work out might not turn out how she wanted. She tried to remember how part of trusting was submitting to God's will when He wanted something different than she did, but now she was hoping that things would work out with Dylan no matter what.

The call with her client was one of those moments of joy in her profession. While she listened to the teary wonder of the author on the other end of the call, she could only remember how much she loved her job. She was living the dream. She knew it. She had told herself over and over that she was living the dream. And finally, in that call, she believed it.

As she rode back to her apartment in a cab, she tried to linger in that joy, but it had flitted away. But she was energized to meet with the acquiring editor to work out the contract.

Dylan still hadn't called back. Would they play phone tag forever? Was that to be their relationship? If they even had one. They weren't even a thing. They'd kissed. They'd talked. She'd visited him and his family. Kate sighed. What a family. She loved the Dawsons. And they seemed to love her. Or they loved everyone and that's just how they were. Maybe everyone felt that special in their home. She didn't know. She couldn't know. She was not like Shelby, practically raised there. She had no past with them to fall back on.

Shelby never called either, but she had texted a quick update. Her mother was awake, and she seemed like she would be fine. Miraculously fine. But Shelby gave no indication when she would be returning to New York.

Kate imagined her there, with Dylan working and training nearby. And she put the thought out of her mind. No wonder Kate and Dylan were playing phone tag. He had other things and other people in his life right now. Not just Shelby, she amended. His family lived close, and of course the training for a rodeo circuit was intense, she imagined. Well, she had enough to occupy her time. If the typical standard contracts were anything to go by, she might make a significant amount of money from this new deal. Maybe enough to rent a place by the park.

Her phone rang. *Shelby.* "Hey, friend."

"Kate! The best things are happening. I have to tell you or I'm going to scream!"

"Your mom is better, I'm guessing?" Kate smiled.

"Oh yes, didn't I tell you? She's coming home today. She

needs to rest and take some new meds, but she should be fine. My dad is so relieved." She paused a moment. "But I have news!"

"Oh?" Kate braced herself.

"Yes! I was just offered a job here at home."

"What?" Kate laughed. "Are you gonna take it?"

"Well, why not? Don't you think I should?"

No, she did not think Shelby should work in Willow Creek. But that was just selfishness talking. "I thought you loved New York."

"Well, I do of course, but you saw me at home. I fit in here. I'm happier. Dylan is here…"

Kate had nothing to say to that.

"But I'm not selling my rental contract yet."

If Shelby moved out, the new roommate could be anyone. Kate pulled up real estate websites.

"Kate?"

"Oh. Sorry. I'm looking around for new places too."

"You are?" The accusation in her tone rubbed at Kate.

"Well, sure, if you don't come back." Kate didn't want to deal with this right now.

"You could get along with anyone. I wouldn't worry about that. But, Kate, Dylan was so sweet the other night. We went out back on the porch swing and just watched the moonrise. It's a funny Dawson tradition, you know." She giggled, and Kate wanted to hang up. "And we talked through some things. We talked about you."

Kate sucked in her breath. "Oh?"

"Well, yeah. He was so grateful he met you, and you helped him through a tough spot."

She made it sound like things were over. Kate didn't want to be having this conversation. "I'm glad to hear it. Hey, Shelby. I've got a client waiting for a contract. Can I call you later?" Or never.

"Oh sure. Hey, I'll come see you again if I decide to take this job. It might depend a lot on how things progress with Dylan. He doesn't ever stay put, does he?"

"Yeah, I don't know. Good to talk to you. Bye."

She hung up and closed her eyes. Was this how she would hear Dylan had moved on? Through Shelby's hints and subtext? She couldn't handle this right now.

She turned off her phone and began putting together everything she would need for her upcoming meeting.

KATE WALKED out of the New York offices of Penwich Publishing, trying not to skip in happiness. In her heels, she would have fallen down, and it just wasn't professional, but wow. She'd just signed the biggest deal of the year for her client. The biggest! Her grin grew.

"Good news?" A man, tall, young, and with a grin to melt any heart stood at a newspaper stand with coffee in hand, watching her.

"Oh, yes. The best kind." She was giddy.

"This calls for a celebration."

"I was just thinking the same thing."

"Can I buy you lunch?"

"Yes. That's just what I want right now."

"Excellent." He held up a hand, and a yellow cab stopped. "Can I take you to my favorite place?"

"Hmm. Surprise me." She hopped in the cab with him and then laughed. "Uh, I'm Kate."

He took her hand and cradled it more than shook it. "Very nice to meet you, Kate. I'm Spencer. You have such a happy energy. I could use a little bit of that. Thanks for letting me take you to lunch."

"Where are we going?"

"Have you ever eaten at the top of the Waldorf?"

So expensive. "No."

"Then the Waldorf it is. It's the perfect place for celebrations. And the Christmas decorations should be up."

"Oh, that's wonderful. Thank you." She sat back, a little bit uncomfortable. Perhaps the giddy spontaneity should have been thought through. She might have preferred a walk in the park as her celebration. But hopefully things wouldn't be too awkward.

"So, tell me your news. Is it something you can share?"

Her grin grew. "Yes. Not the details, but I just signed a deal for an author that will make literary headlines tomorrow."

His eyes sparkled. "Ah, and so I heard it first."

"Yes. You did. It's everything I ever dreamed for in this job."

"What agency are you with?"

She told him, and he nodded. "I work in finance. So this sits far outside my world."

"Yes, it does. What are you doing all the way up here on your lunch break?"

"I didn't go in today. I too have a bit of news."

"What is it?"

"I just signed a consulting deal that might make the headlines tomorrow as well."

"Well that's excellent! So we are celebrating us both."

They pulled up to valet parking. As soon as she walked in the door, she was pleased they were there. The lobby had a lovely traditional Christmas tree. The deep, rich wood, the thick carpets, the dim lighting, and the lovely banisters all told Kate this was a great idea. "I love Christmas in New York."

"Are you staying here over the holidays?"

"Yes, I think so." She didn't have anywhere else to go.

He led her up the stairs and to a second-floor elevator. It looked fancy and just old-fashioned enough for Kate to love it even more. When they exited out on the very top floor, she gasped at the completely glassed in space. "This is gorgeous."

"Not many people know about this." He stopped at the hostess table. "Thankfully."

They were immediately shown to a table next to the window. A tree in the middle of the restaurant and the soft Christmas music played on a piano somewhere made her smile and set her at ease.

"So, tell me, Spencer. How long have you lived here in New York?"

As he talked, his white teeth practically gleamed at her. His sharp jawline and bright flashing blue eyes would have attracted many a woman. He was charming and polite and obviously successful. He filled his suit jacket in just the right ways. But nothing dazzled her. In the middle of his story about a funny cab driver, she was distracted by thoughts of Dylan and his truck. She'd love to see him drive that huge thing around Manhattan.

"And now I've lost you."

"What? No, I'm sorry. This has been a big day. I'm still with you. But I wonder if you might have some suggestions. I'm thinking of moving to a new apartment in the Upper West Side. Do you have a suggestion?"

"My brother. He's a real estate agent and lives up there." He lifted a card out of his wallet. "That's him. Tell him I sent you."

"Thank you." She slipped the card in her purse. The more she thought about it, the more she wanted her own space, and she wanted space by the park. She didn't want to admit it, but she missed the land, the green all around the Dawson farm. She craved it now that she'd come back.

As they left the Waldorf, he stepped closer. "I think I'd like to get to know you better."

She nodded, considering him. "Call me." She handed him her phone.

"Excellent." He grinned into her camera and then handed back the phone just as her cab arrived.

"Thank you for lunch. That was just what I needed."

"I'll look for you in the headlines tomorrow."

"And I'll look for you." She stepped inside, waved her phone at him, and then drove away. She gave the driver her address and leaned back with a sigh. A couple months ago, that would have been the best thing to happen in a long time, especially after the amazing book deal. He was, by all appearances, amazing. Had Dylan ruined her for any other man? As she thought about his smile, his eyes, and the way she felt when she was with him, she knew she'd never feel the same about another man, at least not for a while.

The late November air was crisp but unseasonably warm, so she asked the driver to let her out early. "I'll walk a few blocks." The decorations were up. The lights were strung. As soon as it got dark, the wonderland feel would have returned.

Weeks went by and she still hadn't heard from Dylan. She tried to call him a few times, leaving messages, but when he didn't answer at all, she gave up. He was still a part of many of her thoughts, but what could she do? She'd signed five more authors and was just about to sign papers on a new condo overlooking the park. Everything seemed to be going just as it should. She guessed Dylan was beginning his national rodeo tour. He had said something about November. She guessed Shelby had decided to stay home, because she hadn't heard from her in a long time either.

Then one day, on a walk outside her apartment, she noticed a tall man with broad shoulders and boots out of the corner of her eye. She turned so fast she startled the man, who was standing next to her on the sidewalk. "Decker?"

"I was wondering when you were gonna notice me over here."

She stepped into his arms, squeezing him tight. "How could I miss you? Wow it's good to see you. What are you doing here?"

"I'm out here on business."

"What? Really!"

"Yeah. Maybe Dylan told you. I was working on some ideas out here a few years ago."

"I remember something like that. Hey, come on up. I want to hear how everyone is."

"I have a minute. Want to go grab some food?"

"Should I just order in?" Something about Decker Dawson called for a kitchen table and a good chat.

"Well, sure. That sounds great."

"Where are you staying?"

"Just right across the street."

Right where Dylan had stayed.

CHAPTER 23

*D*ylan was dying inside.

Shelby clung to his arm while they walked down the Dawson property line. Her voice chattered away, rising up and down in excitement. "And then she told me, no way, but I knew she was going to go down on price. She just had to. Who sells their used purse for the same price as brand new? I don't care what the label says…" Shelby talked of her shopping more often than not. She missed New York and had found knock-off purses online.

Dylan had lost track of exactly what she was doing. She worked in town. but as far as Dylan could tell, she was never at her job. She spent most of her days and nights hanging around the fairgrounds watching him train. She'd taken up residence in his trailer too, in the daytime only. He'd expressed to her time and again his rules about evening visitors, meaning he didn't want any.

Isn't this what he wanted, though? A woman with him on the road? Shelby was setting up her life so she could be that. Her mother was doing much better. And her parents were happy to have Shelby at home again as far as Dylan could tell.

They had stopped talking about Kate. At first, Shelby told him Kate needed her space. She was in the middle of a huge deal and that's why she hadn't called him. And he saw her online. He'd googled her name and saw she had signed a huge contract and then several others right after. He was happy for her. But he wished they were talking. Why weren't they talking?

He scrolled through his recent calls again. She was on there as missed calls, but no voicemails. How could that be? He'd left her enough. At first. He clicked on deleted messages. "Wait, what?" She'd left two. Three weeks ago. And somehow they'd been deleted. He put his phone up to his ear and stepped away from Shelby, no longer hearing or seeing her.

Kate's voice made him smile. "Hey, cowboy. Hope you got my note. I've got some good news from work and some things to hurry and work on. Looked like you'd be busy for a long while anyway. Thanks for the weekend."

He clicked on the next message. "Hey, Dylan. I haven't heard from you. I hope things are going well. I think about you getting ready to ride, and I wish you the best. Everything is great here. I guess things are the way they're meant to be, right? Even though that seems true, I still miss you. Call me."

He groaned. When was that? Two weeks ago. "Two weeks!"

"What? What is it?" Shelby tugged on his arm, but he shook his head.

"I missed a voicemail from Kate. Two weeks ago."

"Oh, don't worry about that. She knows how things are."

He stopped. "What do you mean she knows how things are?"

"Oh, you know, like we're talking. I'm here now, practically living at the rodeo grounds..." Her voice trailed off. "Dylie, come on. I didn't want her to keep holding onto some kind of hope about the two of you. Girls fall hard for someone like you. But how would you ever make it work?"

"That's not for you to decide." He stepped away. "Hey, I've got a call to make, do you mind walking yourself back today?"

Her face pinched, but she nodded. "Sure. Right." She took two steps and then came back. "Dylan, look, I know we are just barely getting back together, we're tentative. I know we have some things to work out. I didn't treat you very well when I was in New York, but I think we have a good thing going. I wouldn't want to mess that up with a maybe."

He hardly heard her. "Thanks, Shelby." With his phone up to his ear again, he waited for Kate to pick up.

But she didn't.

He left her a message. "Kate. Man, Kate. I miss you. I'm standing here behind the house, looking out over the valley and the house, and all of it is as beautiful as ever. But it just doesn't mean anything to me anymore. Anyway, I don't want to leave a long, sappy message, but call me. Forgive me for missing these voicemails from you."

When he pocketed the phone, he took off at a run. He needed to get back to pack up his stuff. They were going on the road tomorrow. His first two rodeos had been right there in San Antonio and Houston, but now he was heading to Ohio. And from there, all over the country. Maybe he could stop by to see Kate in New York. His heart picked up. Just knowing that she wasn't ignoring him made all the difference.

But she would think he had been ignoring her. A woman could make a lot of decisions based off of simple things like being ghosted.

His walk turned to a jog, all the way back to the ranch house.

When he stepped in the door, Mama met him with a hug. "Just heard from Decker. Guess where he is!"

He followed her into the living room, where Decker's large face was up on the TV. Nash was FaceTiming him, and Gracie was trying to tell him something. Dylan stopped moving halfway into the room. "Is that..." He wasn't sure, but it looked a lot like Kate's kitchen.

"Is that my unholy twin?"

"Deck! Where are you?"

"Oh, just visiting our favorite New Yorker." He moved his phone, and then Kate's face filled their television. His heart rose up to his throat, and he took two steps toward the TV before Nash punched him in the shoulder. "Dude, you talk into the phone."

"Oh right." He felt his own face heat, and then he was looking into Kate's face on the phone. "Kate."

"Hi." Her smile was large and open. But her eyes held insecurity and questions.

"I just left you a message."

"You did?" She looked down at her phone. "Ah, look at that. I haven't seen a single notification from you in weeks."

"I know. I'm so sorry. I didn't even know you'd called. My voice messages were erased." He frowned, suddenly suspicious. "Tell me how you've been. Have you been to the park? I saw you on Google. You've signed all these deals." He stopped, worried Shelby was starting to rub off on him.

"I'm great. It's been amazing. Everything I've ever wanted here in New York has suddenly happened all at once."

"That's so good. Like someone knew you'd better get it all done at once, right?"

She smiled and then her eyes lit. "Yeah, maybe something like that." She nodded. "Like, if I wasn't going to be here forever, kind of thing?"

"I don't know, maybe that kind of thing. Or maybe a wait and see kind of thing. I start my national tour soon, but that leaves some weekdays open here and there. Maybe I can come back and visit again?"

She didn't answer for a second longer than felt comfortable, then her quiet voice said, "Dylan, what is this?"

He nearly choked on the sadness in her eyes. "I'm so sorry that you even have to ask that question. What is this? This is me,

Kate, asking for you to be in my life 'cause I don't like my life without you in it. I don't even like the rodeo if we're not talking. I knew it would be sad to be apart, but I don't know how to be physically together every day. That might not even be the best thing right now, but let's talk. I can't have us not talking."

"I can meet you halfway." Her smile started small but grew.

He couldn't believe she was talking to him, that they were planning to meet. "Really?"

She laughed and then Nash's snickers became audible. He turned. The whole family, of course, was listening to every bit of their conversation as they watched it on the large screen television. "Just a second, Kate." He switched the settings and stopped sharing the call. "Really, dude."

"I heard everything on my end, too. Anybody get that on video?" Decker's voice from Kate's phone reminded him that his brother was sitting right there next to Kate.

"Oh, don't you worry about them. They'll understand someday, and then there might be some sweet moments of revenge for you." Mama smiled and then looked into the phone. "Kate, darling. We all miss you around here—not just this lovesick cowboy here, all of us."

"Thank you, Mama Dawson. I miss you too."

He almost hated to do it, for fear they wouldn't talk again. "Hey, Kate, I'm loading up the truck to hit the road this weekend. Can I call you in an hour?"

Decker took back over the screen. "Better yet, dude, we're gonna meet you there."

"What!"

Kate laughed. "Where we going?"

"Ohio. You got time for that?"

Decker grinned. "We're getting on the plane in a few hours. I already got us tickets."

"You did?" Dylan and Kate asked at the same time.

"Sure did. You two just sit tight, I got this all figured out."

Dylan wanted to hug his brother right then and there. But he just grinned and said thank you. He wanted to linger on the call, staring into Kate's face, but he resisted since his family was still watching and hung up.

"Well, isn't that something." Nash sat back on the couch with his arms behind his head.

Dylan ignored his razzing. "She did call."

"Of course she called, honey. And didn't I talk to you about having a little trust?"

"That, Mama, is easier said than done."

"You're still gonna need a good dose of trust, you know? It's not like you two are neighbors or anything."

"But now that I know what it's like to live apart and silent, I can do apart if we're talking." He stopped. "Maybe that's something I needed to learn."

"Maybe." Mama's wise face made him grin. "I suspect there are a few more things you picked up along the way, too."

"I bet you're right. Like that Shelby just isn't right for me."

Nash held up a finger and nodded.

"Now, honey, does Shelby know this?"

"She does, but I'll tell her in a few different ways."

"Can I tell her?" Nash shook his head. "I got a feeling she's gonna need to hear it straight."

"No, Nash. You let Dylan take care of this."

"I'm good if Nash reinforces the idea, on repeat." Dylan laughed.

Nash nodded. "I got you covered, brother. Now get on out of here so you can see your woman smiling at you from the family seats."

His heart thumped and he stood taller. "From the family seats." He kissed Mama on the cheek and raced out the door, whistling for Sam.

The dog bounded into the truck like he'd been waiting to be called. "Time to get ourselves a girlfriend." Dylan pulled out of the driveway. "Time to get ourselves a wife." A feeling of peace filled the front of the truck. Kate. His now. His future. "Thank you." His whisper to heaven was as heartfelt as any prayer.

CHAPTER 24

$\mathcal{K}$ ate sat in the stands next to Decker, waiting for the show to start. A whole row of chairs sat open in front of them. "I wonder who's coming, hopefully no one tall."

Decker grinned. "I think I see them now."

"Who?" She followed his gaze. The whole Dawson clan filed into that row, coming from down on the other end. Maverick and Nash towered over everyone. They had on their Dawson Ranch T-shirts. And people started to notice. Maverick was stopped a lot, and Nash sometimes too. They nodded and grinned and shook some hands, with Mama Dawson smiling broader than Kate had ever seen her smile. Gracie skipped along with Bailey at the end of the line. She pointed out things here or there across the way.

"They're all really here?"

"Yep, Dylan is important to us. And you are, too." He smiled. "Welcome to the family, Kate. No matter what happens with you guys, you'll always be one of us."

"I like the sound of that." She grinned.

She stood as they filed in front of her, and she hugged each one. The love she felt surround them all was really something special. "We going out for dinner after?"

"You know it." Nash tipped his hat. "Now, we've got to do something about your shirt." He tossed her a Dawson Ranch shirt, and she slipped it over her head.

"That's more like it."

"I completely agree."

Everything seemed too good to be true. "How's Shelby?" she asked the group. She half expected her to show up any second with a drink and fries.

Mama Dawson answered. "She's doing okay. She and Dylan had a nice long conversation, and she agreed to give you two some space."

"And I'm in charge of reinforcing the message." Nash sat taller and winked. "I've got it taken care of."

Kate blushed. "I feel a little sheepish..."

Nash shook his head. "Nope. Don't you be feeling anything but pleased as a pig in mud. You are the best thing to happen to Dylan, and that's the truth of it."

"That was sentimental." Decker nudged Nash.

"What can I say?"

The announcer began his opening, and Kate sat forward in her seat.

One event after another showed some amazing talent. Then the ropers started, and Kate had never seen so many good participants. To her, they all did equally well, except for the couple who failed to tie down the calf. "How do they know who wins?"

"The judges are watching everything. Timing plays a huge role. He has to beat the world record in order to win."

"What? Wow."

"Yep. That guy just now tied it."

"Can Dylan do it?"

"Yep. He's the one who holds it." Decker's proud grin made her love the family even more.

"Well, okay then. I know he was working on his times last I was there."

"That's why. He's broke the record in practice. Let's all of us keep our fingers crossed."

Mama turned to them. "And pray."

"I don't know if God wants to hear us asking about winning a rodeo." Nash shook his head.

"If we care, He cares. And we care." Mama clasped her hands together. "You know all the publicity brings money to the ranch."

"Yeah, alright." Nash bowed his head.

Kate looked on in amazement. "Is he gonna pray right here?"

"Sure as rain." Decker turned back to the arena.

Nash looked up and winked. "I think Dylie's next."

Kate snorted. "I am not calling that man Dylie."

"Praise the hogs for that." Nash offered his knuckles.

The announcer called out, "Next up. Dylan Dawson from the Dawson Ranch. Dylan is our world record holder for this event and the top pick to win."

Decker pointed. "He's right over there, but you can't see him."

She sent her gaze his way. Her love poured out of her. And her prayers lifted to heaven. As soon as he tore out onto the arena floor, his rope high in the air with Pepper racing after the calf, she knew she'd never seen anything that beautiful. He swung the rope in a circle once, twice, and sent it flying toward the calf. It caught and jerked the calf to a stop. Pepper pulled back. Dylan raced over, kneeled to the ground, and tied up the hooves faster than she could count. Then he stood and pointed directly at their group.

All the Dawsons and Kate stood up, screaming and jumping in their seats. The time flashed on the board.

"He's done it!" the announcer shouted into the speakers. The crowds cheered like crazy. "Dylan Dawson has done it again. By a full half second. You are looking at the new world record. You saw it here, folks."

Dylan circled the arena with his hands in the air and then slowed right in front of their group. His eyes bored into hers. She placed a hand on her heart. Then he tipped his hat once and took off out of the arena.

"Oh." She fell back against her seat. "Wow."

"And that's what a woman's got to do for me someday." Nash eyed her. "Do you think she will?"

"Of course she will." Mama reached over and patted his hand.

"Thanks, Mama. From the words of my own mother."

The Christmas music started up, and the clowns came out. Kate kept peering into the darkness where Dylan had gone.

"Should we tell him to get hisself out here?"

"Can he?" Kate asked.

"They don't usually, but I don't think he's competing in anything else."

But then Dylan came riding back out, Pepper decorated in ribbons. Dylan switched out his usual hat for a stiffer, cleaner version or at least it looked like it from there.

"Dylan Dawson back out on the sand with an announcement to make."

"What?"

They all watched him, with Kate holding her breath. He held up a microphone and rode slowly around, waving to the crowd, until he stood in front of their group. "There's a woman here tonight that flew in from New York to see me. Can I get some cheers for Kate?"

People craned their necks to look in her direction. People clapped and cheered politely. And then her image went up on the screen with the words, *Will you be my girlfriend?*

The crowd erupted in cheers.

"I know we live apart. I know I'll be in a new place every weekend, but I can't live without you. Kate, what do you say?"

Decker pushed her forward, and Mama pulled from the front. She stepped out across their row and stood at the rail in front of him.

"Hey."

"Hey yourself."

He looked good, real good. And it was all she could do to keep herself from climbing out on his horse.

"Wanna go for a ride?"

"What? Right now?"

He nodded. "Yep."

"Totally."

Her pulled her close, and she breathed in the smell of him. His lips met hers, and the crowd went crazy. Pepper started to move, but they didn't even mind. When at last they stopped and she turned to face the crowd, he laughed into his microphone. "I think that was a yes!" He lifted his hat into the air, and everyone cheered again.

They rode around one more time and then headed backstage.

"Am I allowed back here?"

"You are now."

She turned back. "I missed you."

"I can't even talk about it. I don't even want to see the rest of this thing. Are you here the whole weekend?"

"I think so. I can be."

"Good."

They rode back through the fenced-off area, toward what looked like some indoor stalls. "Let's get Pepper situated, and then we have some catching up to do."

"I have so much to tell you."

"Well, yeah, but I was thinking of the other kind." He wiggled his eyebrows at her until she swatted at him. But she didn't mind one bit.

As soon as Pepper was in his stall, he handed her a brush. "Help me brush him down?"

They stepped in together, but as soon as the door shut, he pulled her into his arms. With Pepper at her back and Dylan in front, pulling her close, she didn't think anything could be sweeter. Her lips responded to his urgency with an intensity she'd never known. Over and over, he kissed her and she responded. His arms circled around her, and she didn't know how to get closer. Dylan was back. He wanted her. She was his girlfriend. At that thought, she almost squealed. Her smile was obvious, and Dylan paused. "You happy about something?"

"Cowboy, I've never been happier."

"Just what I like to hear."

**

If you haven't read Coming Home to Maverick, book one in this series, continue to read Chapter one next. You can purchase a copy HERE.

Book THREE in the series Loving Decker is available for preorder HERE

CHAPTER ONE, COMING HOME TO MAVERICK

$\mathcal{M}$averick dipped his hat lower against the hot Texas sun. A man's hat could hide a lot of things, unfortunately not everything. His forearms flexed against the rough wood of the split-rail fence, as he stretched his fingers open and closed. His mind was so far away he hardly noticed Colton or the new horse in the small corral used for training horses. This new colt was fighting every effort to break him, and Maverick didn't blame him one bit. He knew his thoughts were ridiculous, but he suddenly wanted that horse on the run, leaping over the fence and taking off across the pasture. Their new trainer was having a devil of a time with the Spawn of Satan, and Maverick wanted to see who would break first— Colton, the trainer, or Spawn, his horse. His bets were on Colton. The horse had passion, fire, and a strong will, exactly what Maverick needed in himself right now.

The tension in the horse's flank, his flared nostrils, and the dance of trainer and horse were familiar, comforting. Maverick imagined himself out there, facing the whip, as he tried to distract himself from the shattering news of a just a few hours ago.

Their property, which stretched for miles in every direction, had always felt like a safe haven. He'd felt God in those hills countless times. But even the stark beauty of the rugged, rocky terrain and rolling green hills couldn't protect him from the news that had sent him out riding the fence line, checking their bales of hay, inspecting the tractors in the back barn, and then finally here to the horse paddock. He'd tried to send some prayers up to Heaven on the way, but at least that afternoon, God was being strangely silent.

His phone rang. "Yeah."

"Where are you?" Dylan's gruff voice made him smile.

"You worried about me?"

"I'm more worried about the paperwork I gotta send to the accountant."

Maverick didn't believe that for a second. "Colton needed some support."

The quiet on the line said more than any response could have. Maverick was hiding. They all knew it.

Maverick grunted. "And I needed some space."

"So you heard."

"How could I not hear when no one can stop talking about it?"

"You coming in for lunch?"

The whole family gathered for lunch every day. It was more like a late breakfast, but it was a family rule that they show up. And for the first time in a long time, Maverick wished he could avoid them, at least for a little while longer. The last time had been when they'd laid their father to rest in the family plot on the northwest corner of their property. His father had been his hero; he'd raised four boys into men, created a successful thriving ranch, and left the Dawson Ranch legacy to Maverick.

And now Maverick's fiancée had returned after six years, with no explanation, no effort to reach out. She just showed back up in their hometown. And he found himself needing some solitude.

Spawn kicked up his back legs and leapt around the paddock, trying to rid himself of the newly placed saddle. Maverick envied the horse. When would it ever be acceptable for Maverick to kick up his heels and buck off whatever he didn't want to deal with?

But he knew he'd best be heading back to the kitchen, or he'd suffer the wrath of Mama. And no one with any sense or brains messed with his mama. He grinned. They owed everything to the strength of that very short woman. "I'll be there."

He heard a grunt of approval or relief or something—who knew what Dylan's grunts meant—and then he hung up the phone. His gaze traveled over the surrounding hills, the patchwork green and tan of the hay they put out every year to feed the livestock. In a couple months, they'd be bringing in the cows to sell at auction. They'd harvest their crops and nestle in for the winter months. The guys would start in on the rodeo circuit, Mama would participate in the local craft shows and fairs, and he'd take a break.

He hopped on the ATV, waved good luck to Colton, who was being controlled by the young horse, and then took the longest path back to the house.

He offered a prayer as he crested the ridge overlooking his family's homestead. "Thank you Lord for all the goodness in our lives, for my brothers and my Mother." He paused, expecting a rush of satisfaction. They'd built something special. The Dawson brothers were known for their cattle, their horses, and their rodeo championships. His father would be proud. They were all fine, honorable men. And according to Dad, that's what mattered. "I don't care what career you choose," he used to say, "but be honest, hardworking, and competent at whatever it is."

Except in Maverick's case, Dad did care what he became. Maverick was the new head of the Dawson Ranch, the new head of the family, as prescribed in the will his father left. Only, Maverick felt like half the man his father had been. He turned the ATV back down the path. His other brothers were pulling up to the house. Time for lunch. He finished his prayer. "I should be grateful, and I am. Help me to show it today even though I've had some hard news." He grit his teeth, knowing he should say the next words, but finding it difficult. "And please bless Bailey. She must have gone through an awful lot. Amen."

A loud, musical horn echoed across the valley, and he shook his head. Nash. Sounded like his youngest brother was in high form. His Jeep spun out in the gravel at the start of the long drive, and then he slowed to a crawl as he approached the house. Maverick nodded to himself. Nash knew better than to throw dust all over Mama's flowers. Mama was continually reminding them that someday they'd have grandkids running around the front yard and they'd all have to be careful.

Grandkids. Maverick had stopped counting how old his kids would have been if he and Bailey had actually been married. They could have had two by then. Or maybe they would have had a long honeymoon relationship with no children. He'd have liked that just as well.

"Stop," he told himself again. Bailey's return to Willow Creek had brought back emotions he thought he'd buried years ago. But pieces of his heart still longed for her and felt as raw as the day she left. Before he could shut out the memory, the view of the long aisle at the church filled his mind—the pews decorated with ribbons and flowers, the floor sprinkled with flower petals. Everyone they knew and loved smiling up at him, his mother's eyes full of tears, and his father's full of pride. He swallowed the lump in his throat before it could turn into anything that would make his eyes red when he walked into lunch with his family.

He drove down the side of the hill and parked his ATV in the garage, wiping off the trail dust and placing the keys on the hook. Then he went through the workroom, tidying the few items out of place. He brushed the dust off himself again, wiped his face, and ran a hand through his hair. His hat went on a hook—no hats at the dinner table. He was about to open the door into the house when his mama's voice stopped him.

"We love you, son. We'll support you in whatever you want to do."

He turned to face her. Her hair was still damp from her shower, the soft curls framing her face. She stood near the entry into the house, watching him, seeing through his stoic front. Mama was a dear, but she had no notion of the private emotions of a man's heart.

"What I want to do?"

Her eyes were kind with a hint of sorrow, and he hated that he was the cause. She handed him some napkins to bring in from the storage room and a bin for extra dishes.

He'd endlessly analyzed the events of his wedding day and he and Bailey's relationship, and still he couldn't imagine how he could have acted differently. And he didn't know what more he could do now. You can't prepare to be blindsided. And he knew his mama had been hurt in her own way. She'd given her heart to Bailey and had, in some ways, lost a daughter when the woman had left.

Mama nodded. "Yes. We're with you whatever you decide to do—or not do."

He wrapped an arm around her. "I don't know what I want to do. But I do know I love you, Mama. Let's go have some of Cook's food."

She laughed. "The best thing you ever did was hire a cooking staff."

"I see no reason why you have to be the one to make your signature hotcakes."

"Sometimes I go make sure they've got it right," she said with a smile.

"I have no doubt. And they're delicious every time."

She stood on tiptoe. He dipped his head so she could kiss his cheek and give it a pat. "You're a good man, Maverick. You deserve to be happy."

"I am, Mama. What more could a dusty cowpoke need?"

She wiped her hands on the front of her apron and then took it off. She placed it on a hook, and together they entered the house and made their way into the large dining room. Maverick stood in the doorway. All three of his brothers were in town, and each of them sat at the table. Heaping piles of pancakes waited on platters down the center of the table. Almost as much bacon, eggs, toast, and thick slices of ham made his stomach grumble. Instantly, his mood lifted.

"Brothers." He nodded. No one heard him.

Nash stood from his chair. "You can't even go there. If I'm riding Spice, no one's gonna beat me. Not you, not Tommy, no one."

"You're a mess, Nash."

"Take a look in the mirror before you go making comments, Decker. When's the last time you brought home a first place?"

Mama cleared her throat and nodded toward the sign on the wall behind her. "Dawson happiness starts at home."

The brothers grumbled but closed their mouths.

Mama treated this room as the center of their family. She kept their portraits in there, their senior pictures from high school. The wall also held two phrases the family lived by. "If you're unhappy, get to work" was displayed in large sweeping letters on the opposite wall from the one Mama had just quoted. The brothers stood when Mama entered. She sat at the head of the huge, thick wood table that dominated the room. Then her eyes turned to Maverick, alerting his brothers to his presence.

"Hey, Maverick! How's the colt?" Dylan asked. He was the one who took care of the horses, including their training and breeding.

Maverick felt their eyes on him as he moved to sit at the

other end of the table. "He lives up to his name. Good test run for Colton, though you're gonna have to save him. Maybe sooner than later."

Dylan nodded. "He'll come around. They both will. Colton came highly recommended. He has a way with horses like no one I've ever seen."

Maverick was grateful they were talking business. "Nash, I heard your new horn."

"Isn't it awesome!" he said, his grin wide. "I'm taking the Jeep with me when the circuit starts."

"You're going this year?" Mama poured herself some water.

Everyone looked at their mother as Nash nodded. "Of course, I'm going. You said if I finished out two years helping on the ranch, I could spend the next doing the rodeo circuit."

Mama didn't answer. And she avoided Maverick's gaze. If no one else stayed, Maverick was the one who stayed. And so far, he'd been happy with that. He didn't have a problem with taking over for his father; he'd always known some day he would; he'd just thought it would be later. There's nothing else he would rather be doing anyway, he told himself.

Decker, Dylan's twin, usually disagreed with everything Nash said on principle. But he sat quietly, which Maverick found suspicious.

"What are the predictions on the team this year?"

Mama held up a hand. "Wait. Before we get into all that, let's pray."

Everyone waited for Mama to say a few words. "You know I'm proud of you boys. We miss those not with us, your father most of all, but I know he'd be even more proud of every one of you. Thank you for what you give to the ranch. It's a huge endeavor. Your father gave everything he had to this ranch, knowing it would help take care of each of us for as long as we took care of it." Her eyes traveled to each man at the table, and Maverick knew she desperately needed the ranch. He supposed he did too. It was the only thing they had left of their father. If the ranch lived, their father did too. Mama closed her eyes. They held hands around the table and bowed heads.

"Dear Lord bless this family. Bless this land. Bless the women my boys are going to one day marry. And today especially bless Maverick. We're grateful for every thing in our lives that you placed there in such a perfect way, the hard times and the easy. Amen."

They all echoed, "Amen."

Nash raised his fork. "Let's eat!"

Mama nodded. "Let's eat."

Everyone dug in. Maverick slapped away Decker's hand as he reached for the same slice of ham. "Wait your turn."

Nash passed him a dripping, sticky syrup pitcher.

"Hey now, whoa. Go wipe that off," Maverick said.

"Why me?"

Decker snorted. "'Cause you're the one who drizzled syrup all over the handle."

Nash frowned but got up from the table to wipe the sticky drips of syrup off the handle. The Dawsons had no patience for anything sticky.

They'd almost finished the meal when Decker put down his napkin and looked directly at Maverick. "So, what are you gonna do about Bailey?"

Everyone went silent, and the air thickened with expectation. His mother avoided his eyes, but all three pairs of his brother's eyes waited for his response.

"I don't know that there is anything to do."

"What if she comes walking back in, thinking there's still a chance over here?" Decker's eyes flashed with anger.

"I don't think there's any chance of that. She hasn't said a word to me."

Everyone seemed to be waiting for him to say something else about it. So finally, he sat back in his chair. "I don't know, all right. I had no idea she was coming. I don't know why she left. I don't know what she's been doing except what everyone else knows." He'd stopped checking social media years ago. "So I don't know what to tell you. Will I see her again? I imagine I'll run into her the next time I have to go into town." He tried to keep the pain off his face, but it was just too hard to hide. "I'm not gonna pretend I'm okay with it, but I don't know what else to do except move forward as though we are people that barely know one another."

"We could shun her." Nash twirled his fork. "You know, like outright avoid her, refuse to talk to her. If you asked the town, they'd support you. She hurt them when she left, too." He replaced his fork. "Not as much as you, but they might not want to take her back in with open arms, especially if we say we aren't ready."

Maverick held up his hands. "I don't want us to say or do anything. If we see her, we're polite. If we don't, that's fine too." A part of him wanted to see her right away and get it over with. But the other part wanted to go on a long vacation and hope she left before he came back.

Read the rest HERE.

READ ALL BOOKS BY SOPHIA SUMMERS

JOIN HERE for all new release announcements, giveaways and the insider scoop of books on sale.

Cowboy Inspired Series
Coming Home to Maverick
Resisting Dylan
Loving Decker

Her Billionaire Royals Series:
The Heir
The Crown
The Duke
The Duke's Brother
The Prince
The American
The Spy
The Princess

Read all the books in The Swoony Sports Romances
Hitching the Pitcher

Falling for Centerfield
Charming the Shortstop
Snatching the Catcher
Flirting with First
Kissing on Third

Vacation Billionaires
Holiday Romance

Her Billionaire Cowboys Series:
Her Billionaire Cowboy
Her Billionaire Protector
Her Billionaire in Hiding
Her Billionaire Christmas Secret
Her Billionaire to Remember

Her Love and Marriage Brides Series
The Bride's Secret
The Bride's Cowboy
The Bride's Billionaire